James Otis

With Perry on Lake Erie

A Tale of 1812

James Otis

With Perry on Lake Erie
A Tale of 1812

ISBN/EAN: 9783337073060

Printed in Europe, USA, Canada, Australia, Japan

Cover: Foto ©Andreas Hilbeck / pixelio.de

More available books at **www.hansebooks.com**

BY

JAMES OTIS

AUTHOR OF "THE CHARMING SALLY," "AN AMATEUR
FIREMAN," "JOEL HARFORD," ETC., ETC.

ILLUSTRATED BY

WILLIAM F. STECHER

BOSTON AND CHICAGO
W. A. WILDE COMPANY

WITH PERRY ON LAKE ERIE.

TO THE READER.

Some explanation regarding the method of dealing with facts as set down in this tale should, perhaps, be made. Let it first be understood that no liberty has been taken with the names or movements of those men or boys introduced herein. Much of the incident has been taken from manuscript, the correctness of which cannot be doubted, and all has been verified by reference to our standard histories. In no single instance has any departure been made from the truth, even though the interest of the story might have been increased by a more decided flavor of romance, — notably during the time when the American fleet lay in Presque Isle bay, useless because lacking men.

It seems fitting that Commodore Perry's deeds should be related from the standpoint of that younger brother who shared his troubles as he did his triumphs, whether the same be set forth as reading for adults, or young people ; because it must be admitted that he who won such a glorious victory on Lake Erie was hardly more than a boy. Very young people look upon one who has seen twenty-seven years of this world's battle as an elderly person ; but those who have passed the noon of life are prone to speak of such as " lads," and therefore is this essentially a story of young people.

JAMES OTIS.

CONTENTS.

ILLUSTRATIONS.

WITH PERRY ON LAKE ERIE.

A Tale of 1812.

CHAPTER I.

PRESQUE ISLE.

PERHAPS there is no good reason why I should set down here any especial mention of Presque Isle,[1] for every boy knows it is located on the shore of Lake Erie, and, because of the peninsula jutting out from the mainland of the State of Pennsylvania, can boast of an exceedingly good harbor.

It is a lame beginning to the story I want to tell, this opening with the admission that there may be no reason for making a certain statement; but I am not quick at tasks of the kind it is proposed this shall be, and one mistake among the many I shall probably make will not be noticed.

Even now I have failed to begin the yarn to my satisfaction; but I have written and rubbed out so

---

[1] Now known as the city of Erie.

much already, that the lines above must stand as they
are set down, else I may never arrive at the beginning of such a tale as few lads can tell of their own
experience.

That I am making any attempt at doing what nature
fitted me for with such a niggardly hand, is due to
Alexander Perry, brother of that Oliver H. Perry
who proved himself so great a hero here on the
waters of Lake Erie, when he gave the King of England a second and much-needed lesson.   He, meaning
Alec, and I saw much of service in the war so lately
ended with honor to the people of the United States.
Although he was but thirteen years of age, and I only
two years older, we passed through many adventures
together, shared many hardships, and ever remained
close comrades from the day of our first meeting.

The war having come to an end, and we about to
separate after three years of service, he said to me : —

" Dick, it is for you to set down, in such fair script
as you can master, the story of what we have done
these many months past, so that in the years to come
those who live hereabouts may know we were not idle
when the British king provoked this nation past
endurance."

I would have insisted, as is true, that he was better
able to perform the task than I, who had learned but

little in schools, because there were none hereabouts; but the lad declared I was the one above all others to do the work, and here am I, casting about in my mind as to how the tale can best be set down in readable fashion.

Presque Isle, to hark back to the beginning, was the settlement which my father, Captain Daniel Dobbins, decided upon as the proper place in which to build his home, and within a stone's throw of the blockhouse erected by General Wayne after he had whipped the Indians in Maumee Valley, I was born. Here I lived while my father sailed on the lake, becoming known far and wide as the most skilful navigator of Erie's waters, until war was declared, and then I had the satisfaction of calling myself the son of the man who, after having been called to Washington to give advice to the high officials there, was appointed a sailing-master in the navy.

It was in September of the year 1812 that my father received a commission from the Government, and straightway he began building two gunboats, each with a fifty-foot keel, seventeen-foot beam, and a five-foot hold, counting on having them ready for service as soon as the ice should leave the lake.

Ebenezer Crosby was the carpenter in charge of the work, and under him were mustered all the laborers to be found within fifty miles of the settlement. Even boys were hired, I among the number, and all of us youngsters counted on being given a chance to ship as members of the crews when the vessels were launched.

It was on the 27th day of March, in the year 1813, that a young man and a lad drove up to the door of the Erie Hotel in Presque Isle, and we of the village soon came to know that the strangers were brothers, the elder being a captain in the navy, by name Oliver H. Perry, and the other, Alexander, who at once became a dear comrade of mine.

As the only representative of the Government in Presque Isle, my father was summoned to confer with the officer, and quite by chance I was allowed to accompany him to the hotel.

There, while our elders discussed the best means of building such a fleet as might give successful battle to the enemy, who had already made threats as to what would be done when the lake was free from ice, Alec and I made each other's acquaintance.

He told me that his brother, the captain, had been in command of a small fleet of gunboats at the Newport station; but, eager to see more active service, had applied for a command on the lakes. On the first of February, in this same year, he had received orders from the Secretary of the Navy commanding him to report, with one hundred and fifty men, to Commodore Chauncey, then stationed at Sackett's Harbor.

The force was sent ahead in three detachments, and the captain, with Alec, set out in a sleigh through the wilderness. They arrived at Sackett's Harbor on the third of March, and stayed there a fortnight, expecting each day an attack by the enemy. Then Captain Perry was ordered to Presque Isle to push forward the work my father had begun, and thus were we two lads brought together.

Now the gunboats were not the only vessels building by this time. The keels of two twenty-gun brigs and a clipper schooner were laid down near the mouth of Cascade Creek, and a huge quantity of timber had been felled nearabout ready for the workmen. There was no time in which to season the stuff, and I have seen planking bent on the ribs of a brig within four and twenty hours from the fall of the tree. In fact, my father had a small fleet in process of construction, and Captain Perry was pleased to compliment him for his activity and good judgment.

Sixty men had volunteered under Captain Foster to guard the shipyards against a possible attack by the Britishers, and all the workmen were drilled each evening in the manual of arms, therefore our village presented a very lively and warlike appearance.

While Alec was telling me his story, and I explaining to him all I had done in the work of preparation, our elders had decided as to what further steps should be taken. Captain Perry was to go at once to Pittsburg to send on the necessary supplies, while my father would journey to Buffalo in quest of men and ammunition.

So urgent was the need that no time was spent by either of these officers in repose after once a definite plan was formed; but both set out that same night, and Alexander was left in my charge, a fact which made me feel a certain sense of responsibility and much pride.

It would seem as if I had written over-much in my attempt to give whoever may read these pages a fair idea of how we two — meaning Alec Perry and I — came together, and yet a few more lines of dry detail are necessary for a better understanding of what may follow.

At this time our defences consisted of a small battery and a blockhouse on the bluff at the entrance of the harbor; between them and the town were the old French fort and another small blockhouse. Opposite the town, on the peninsula to the westward of Little Bay, stood a third blockhouse, a storehouse and a hospital, which last buildings were erected after we received word that Captain Perry had been sent to Presque Isle. The gunboats were on the stocks in front of the village; while west of the settlement, at the mouth of Cascade Creek, where was a block-house for the protection of the shipyard, the brigs and the schooner were being built.

My home was on the shore of the harbor midway between the old French fort and the first-mentioned shipyard, and there it was Alec Perry lodged, sleeping in the same bed with me on the night after our first meeting.

Before departing on his journey to Buffalo, my father said to me:—

"You and young Perry are not to remain idle while I am away. It is necessary a message be sent the workmen on the Point, and early to-morrow morning you shall set out with it. You should be able to go and return in two hours, now the ice is in such good condition for skating; but I propose that you remain there three days, going out on the lake a distance of eight or ten miles every night and morning to learn if the enemy are abroad. In other words, you two youngsters are to act as scouts during my absence. Do not run unnecessary risks, and in case of a snow-storm you will remain under cover, for I am not minded to hear on my return that you have come to an untimely end."

c

It puffed me up with pride to have such a commission as this, and Alec's eyes glistened as my father spoke, for he was a brave lad, as has since been proven more than once when I have come nigh to showing the white feather.

There was more in the mission, as we two lads understood it, than had been put into words; surely if we could be depended upon to keep watch over the harbor at a time when there was every reason to believe the enemy might be making ready at the mouth of the Niagara River for an attack upon Presque Isle, then for a certainty we might count ourselves the same as having been accepted members of whatsoever crew we chose to join.

There was very little sleep for us on this first night of comradeship, and I believe had either proposed to set out that very hour, the other would have gladly acceded to the proposition. We did succeed, however, in curbing ambition until slumber closed our eyelids, and when my mother awakened me next morning the time for action had arrived.

It was not a difficult matter to borrow a pair of skates in Presque Isle, for there was hardly a person in the village who did not own what, to us on the shore of the lake, was almost indispensable during the winter months.

The ice was in prime condition when we two made ready for the short journey across to the Point, and the preparations consisted of nothing more than buckling on our skates. We wore such clothing as might be needed, and there was no necessity of burdening ourselves with provisions, because the men at the blockhouse would supply us with food as well as lodging.

But for my being unused to this work of writing, and finding it difficult to set down the words in clerkly fashion, I might say much concerning the blockhouse on the Point and its occupants.

There were men of eighty years, and lads younger than Alec, among the party who called themselves the "garrison," and all of them were known to me; therefore it was much like being among kinsfolk to be quartered with them.

During the first two days Alec and I had plenty of company when we glided over the smooth ice, up the lake in the direction of Niagara River, on what we were pleased to call scouting expeditions; and but for the fact that young Perry insisted upon considering himself in the backwoods, we should have gotten on famously with the young members of the garrison.

Alec, however, having just come from Newport, and not yet used to our customs, persisted in speaking of the surroundings as if he believed himself in an uncivilized country, and many of the lads were disgruntled because, as they said, he put on airs.

To this charge Alec is now willing to plead guilty, although at the time I question if he realized how greatly he set himself above us, until after coming to understand that he had much to learn from the people of Presque Isle.

All this may seem trifling matter to set down on the pages of what is intended to be the story of how Oliver Perry made himself famous on Lake Erie; but yet it led us into an adventure which came near costing the country the unfinished vessels that were sadly needed, and us our lives.

Four times had we left the blockhouse, accompanied by a dozen or more lads, and skated ten or fifteen miles up the lake and back. Then our companions, taking offence at some idle words used by Alec, declared they would not set out with us again.

It was a threat which had but little weight with my comrade or myself, since we had a desire to be alone with each other, and on the morning of the third day, when the sky was gray with threatening-looking clouds, we left the blockhouse, counting to return there but once more before going home, for the time set by my father had come to an end.

Whether we should continue this sport of playing at being scouts, we had decided to leave to Noah Brown, a shipwright who came from New York City, and who was in charge of the works at Presque Isle during my father's absence.

"I regret that the lads were offended with my idle words of yesterday; but yet it is pleasant to set out alone with you, Dicky," Alec said, as we skimmed over the smooth ice in such direction as would bring us to the easternmost battery on the opposite shore. "One might think, to hear those in the garrison talk, that we were surrounded by Britishers, and I have been waiting for an opportunity to ask if you believe the enemy to be near at hand."

"Believe it? I know it to be a fact, Alec. The redcoats are in strong force at the mouth of the Niagara, and certain it is that as soon as the ice breaks up, you will see them in such numbers as to make you alarmed for the safety of our works."

"The Britishers outnumbered our people when the independence of this country was gained, but that did not frighten those who wore the Continental uniform."

"Yet there were many dark days then, Alec, and I have heard my grandfather say that often and again did he believe we should be finally whipped into submission. I am unwilling to declare that there are any here who *fear* the result of this war; but yet I could point out twenty as brave men as might be found, who believe that we as a nation are all too weak to take up arms against so powerful a country as England. It is certain that unless our ships are built, launched, and gotten out of the harbor very soon after the ice breaks up, Presque Isle is in great danger of being captured; and that I have heard my father say a dozen times."

"It is strange that the redcoats fail to show themselves," the lad said musingly, as if ready to doubt my statement regarding the nearness of the Britishers.

"Yet you and your brother, while on the way from Buffalo, heard that the enemy knew what was being done here, and was about to make an attack."

"Yes, and Oliver pressed forward hurriedly, fearing lest we might arrive too late. But now, because no movement has been made, I think he is inclined to doubt the correctness of the statement."

At the time Alec made this remark we had covered two-thirds of the distance between Presque Isle and Long Point, having gone directly across the lake toward the Canadian side, and then it was that the snow began to fall.

My comrade was heedless of the danger which

beset us, because ignorant regarding it, and when I proposed that we turn back at once, making all haste to gain the village or the blockhouse, he said in a tone bordering on that of contempt:—

"You may go if you please; but I count on keeping straight ahead until a good view of the enemy's country can be had."

"We are full twenty miles from home, Alec," I replied, giving no heed to his tone, which at another time might have aroused me to anger. "It is thirty miles from Little Bay to Long Point, and you who are unaccustomed to skating such long distances cannot cover it and return in a single day."

"It makes little difference to me if the journey occupies us well into the night, for then we shall be saved the necessity of going back to the blockhouse where those country louts are free to air their supposed wit."

I saw at once that it was useless for me to make any attempt at dissuading him from his purpose by the argument that he could not endure the fatigue, although knowing full well that such was the case, therefore I tried another tack which, with a lad who had lived on the shore of the lake, would have been sufficient.

"In a snow-storm neither you nor I can skate or

walk in a direct line on the ice, and the bravest man in Pennsylvania would hesitate long before making an attempt to travel ten miles after the storm which now threatens has come in good earnest."

"Then we may as well keep on as to turn back," he said, increasing his speed, thus forcing me to renewed exertions, for I was not minded he should run into danger alone.

During ten minutes or more I said all a lad might to dissuade a headstrong comrade from running into such peril as I knew was in store for us, providing we continued straight ahead.

I reminded him that my father's orders for us to remain under cover in case of a snow-storm were positive, and that they would not have been given without good cause. I also suggested that the brother of a captain in the navy should be more careful than another to render due obedience to those who were in command over him, and referred to my father's commission as sailing-master in the navy to show that either of us, while acting as scouts, must look upon him as our superior officer.

To all my arguments and entreaties he had but a single reply : —

"We are nearer the Canadian shore than the American, and there is less danger in going ahead than in returning."

When I urged that by going back we should be among friends, while to continue on was, perchance, to find ourselves in the hands of the Britishers, he accused me of showing the white feather, and repeated the nursery rhyme of the lad who lived in the woods, and was scared by an owl.

I think it was that bit of doggerel which caused me to forget prudence in order that I might prove myself as brave as he, and yet I did but write myself down a fool, as one certainly is who ventures with no good reason into danger.

The snow did not fall in any great volume. It came gently, and with that steadiness which betokens the beginning of a long, severe storm, and yet I skated on by his side, angry with myself for so doing, but lacking the courage to insist upon his going back.

The ice was as smooth as glass; there was not a breath of wind to impede our progress, and I believe we were covering no less than a mile every four or five minutes.

When, as nearly as I could judge, we had continued this mad chase for half an hour, Alec threw himself upon the ice, declaring he must have a breathing spell.

"I'm not up to this work as you are," he said with a laugh, "and therefore am the more easily winded; but when it comes to endurance, you shall see that I am quite your equal. Ten minutes of a rest now, and I will not ask for a second halt until we stand on his Majesty's soil."

"Ay, and what then?" I asked, speaking sharply, for my patience was well-nigh exhausted, to say nothing of the fact that fear was creeping into my heart rapidly. "What will it avail us to stand on his Majesty's soil?"

"Why, simply this, Dicky Dobbins," Alec replied with a hearty laugh. "We shall go back to Presque Isle, among those who are so valiant while at home, and say we have entered the enemy's country and returned in safety. We can also report that there are no redcoats nearabout to disturb the faint-hearted Pennsylvanians."

"It will be a long day before we return, unless this storm clears away very soon, and of that there is no likelihood," I replied moodily. "We are risking our lives — and it is no less than that, I assure you — for nothing but a whim of yours, which, when gratified, is of no benefit."

"If you are taking it so much to heart, Dicky, we'll turn back now," and in a twinkling, as it were,

Alec was the same cheery, honest lad I had believed him to be these two days past; but alas, his cheeriness, and his honesty, and his good comradeship had returned to him too late.

"We must push forward now, for I dare not make the attempt to go back. The Canadian shore should be within four or five miles, and if it please God we'll gain it before the smother thickens."

I think my words, and the tone in which they were spoken, gave the lad a sense of fear for the first time since we had set out. He looked about him with the air of one who suddenly discovers something, and then turning to me said softly, but with a manner that went straight to my heart:—

"I am sorry, Dicky, that I was so foolish. I have led you into this trouble, and you must lead me out; but my word upon it, that from this moment so long as we stay in this portion of the country, I will ever take your advice."

He clasped my hand as if to ask pardon, and at that moment I felt a breath of air from the northeast. The snowflakes were suddenly whirled with that giddy, dancing motion which so bewilders one, telling me how great the danger, and how short a time we had in which to escape.

"Get up," I said almost roughly. "Keep your

wits about you and bend every energy toward going forward in a straight line; for once we become confused, there is little likelihood of our gaining either shore before the cold lulls us to sleep."

Then, and I can hardly realize now how it occurred, before he could rise to his feet it was as if we were completely surrounded by armed men, and it needed not their speech to tell both of us that we were prisoners.

The Britishers were nearer than even I had imagined, and perchance by this mad trick of Alec's, Presque Isle would be captured; for the people there were depending upon us to give an alarm in case the enemy appeared upon the lake.

We had been false to the trust my father reposed in us, and who could say how much of harm to our country might result?

CHAPTER II.

IT is true that when the enemy came into view from amid the whirling snow, Alec's first thought, as he has since told me, was much the same as mine—that we had brought disaster upon our country.

It is nothing of credit that at the time we gave no heed to the peril which menaced; but I here set it down as some slight plea in our favor, that once the mischief had been done we gave no heed to what might come out of it to us.

The snow was falling in such volume, and being whirled so rapidly by the rising wind, that it was impossible to see very far in either direction, and whether we had been surrounded by a regiment of soldiers, or only a squad of a dozen or more, it was impossible to say.

I knew, however, it had been reported that the Britishers were gathering at Port Rowan, and this fact it was which caused our people to believe a descent upon Presque Isle was contemplated.

Now I knew beyond reasonable doubt that these men had come from the first-named place, and a great hope sprang up in my mind that they might have ventured out for the same purpose as had Alec and I — that our capture was the result of an accident.

All these thoughts ran through my mind during the first two or three seconds after the enemy appeared, and before a single word had been spoken on either side.

The party, fully armed and in uniform, wore storm coats, therefore it was impossible, save by his bearing, to distinguish an officer from a private; but Alec and I quickly understood, or believed we did because of not being immediately questioned, that the men were waiting the arrival of a superior.

It was as if a party of dumb people had come together in this fleecy downpour which whirled and danced until one's eyes ached from the ceaseless swirling.

Alec looked meaningly at me, and I understood what he would have said. There was in his glance a warning against our holding converse lest we might betray something of importance to the enemy; but had the lad known me better he would not have thought such a caution necessary.

A boy who has lived on the frontier during such

troublous times as I had known, is not garrulous in the presence of strangers, and when those strangers are known to be enemies, he would be little less than an idiot who should open his mouth unnecessarily.

Well, we two remained in the centre of this silent group while one might have counted thirty, and then the circle was broken to admit a figure, muffled, like the others, to the eyes in a coat of fur, but approaching with such an air of authority that we knew at once he must be in command.

Now it was I noted the fact that none of the Britishers wore skates, and there came into my mind like a flash the knowledge that we must be close ashore, else these men would not thus have ventured out upon the ice.

I also noted, for one who lives much in the forests is quick to observe every trifling detail in a scene, that the officer asked no questions of his men as to where we had been found, or how they chanced to come upon us; therefore I understood that our approach had been known before we were thus made prisoners, and the remainder was easy to guess.

While I had supposed we were half a dozen miles from the Canadian shore, we must have been within view of those on the foreland, and this squad had come out for no other reason than to capture us, a fact which took much of the burden from my mind, for I had feared we were met by the advance guard of a force sent to attack Presque Isle.

"Where do you come from?" the officer asked, in that insolent tone which was usually employed by those holding his Majesty's commission when addressing one from the American border.

There was nothing to be gained by concealing the truth, and I answered the Britisher fairly, save that there was no good reason why I should explain our purpose in being abroad.

"Why have you come on this side of the lake?" he asked, and I replied, yet holding to the truth, but not telling all.

"We were skating, and had ventured so far from home when the snow began to fall, that it seemed safer to continue on than turn back."

"The question I would have answered is, why did you venture to come so near this side at the beginning? You were well over before the snow began to fall."

"Of that we were ignorant, sir," Alec replied, speaking as if in fear; and I observed that his tone gave satisfaction to the valiant Britisher, who was pleased at being able to frighten two lads. "We must have skated faster than we fancied, and I do assure you, sir, that neither of us had any idea how near we were to an enemy."

Up to this point it appeared as if we were like to come off from the adventure in safety, and I was beginning to believe no more harm would accrue to us than that of being sent back through the storm at risk of losing our way, when one of the men whispered to the officer, after which the latter asked sharply of me : —

"Are you the son of that Daniel Dobbins who has trafficked on the lake?"

It was evident that this soldier, whose face I could not see because of the coat-collar which covered it, had recognized me, and I replied with all the boldness it was possible to assume : —

"I am, sir, and therefore you may know of a certainty from whence we come."

It would have been better had I been less talkative, for now both Alec and I understood that the Britisher's suspicions were aroused.

"Where is your father?" he asked sharply.

I would have given much had I been able to reply promptly; but with his question there came into my mind the thought that I might unwittingly betray an important secret, and for the instant speech was well-nigh impossible. Then, after that unfortunate hesitation, I said : —

D

"I do not know, sir."

"Is he not at home?"

"I am unable to say, sir."

"Why? Was he not at home when you left?"

Now it was necessary I should explain that Alec and I had been these past three days at the block-house, and this statement seemed at variance with the one first made.

The Britisher looked at us searchingly for a moment, and then said, much as though speaking to himself:—

"It is evident you lads have something to conceal. I was inclined to believe the story first told; but now it seems wiser to doubt it. Take off your skates," he added harshly, and we had no choice but to obey.

When we were thus made helpless, so far as escape was concerned, the officer gave some order in a low tone to one of the men, after which he wheeled about, walking in the direction where I believed lay the shore, and was soon lost to view amid the falling snow.

"Forgive me," Alec whispered as he pressed my hand, and I understood full well all that was in his mind.

We two were not inclined for conversation; but even though we had been, it was best to remain silent lest yet more suspicions be aroused, and contenting ourselves with a single glance which meant, for my part, that there was no thought of resentment toward my comrade for having led us into these straits, we obeyed the order of our captors to march in advance.

It was not easy to walk on the ice now thickly covered with dry snow, and our progress was by no means rapid ; yet in less than fifteen minutes we were arrived at the shore, and I wondered why it was we had failed to note the fact of being so near the enemy's lines before the storm began.

We pushed on, forced to do so by those in the rear, straight over the outermost end of the Point, where was a well-defined path showing that it had been frequently travelled, until arriving on the opposite side. Then could be seen a dozen or more log huts, lately constructed, as might be told from the chips and branches which covered the snow in every direction.

Now we knew what I would have given much to have told my father. The reports that a force of Britishers were meditating an attack upon Presque Isle were not without ample foundation, for here beyond a peradventure were the quarters of those soldiers who were to be employed in the manœuvre.

As nearly as I could judge from a hurried glance around, there were quarters for fully two hundred men, and I believed that number had already assembled here.

Many soldiers came out of the huts when we arrived, and because no surprise was exhibited by any of them, we again understood that our approach was observed some time before the capture.

If there had been any hope in our minds that we would be treated mildly because of our youth, it was speedily dispelled.

The soldier in charge of the squad which conducted us, and I judged that he might be a sergeant or a corporal, seized us roughly by the arms, literally thrusting us into a small pen — I can give no other name to that place used as a prison — which was built at one end of the hut nearest the shore.

The door of logs was closed and barred behind us.

It was a regular coffin into which we had been introduced, and save for the light that filtered through the chinks of the logs, we would have been in darkness. Our prison measured, perhaps, five feet square, and we had the choice of standing in a bent position, or of throwing ourselves upon the frozen ground carpeted with snow.

"Snug quarters these!" Alec cried with an unsuccessful attempt at cheeriness. "I have always heard it said that his Majesty had no love for those who call themselves Americans, but never before knew he would vent his displeasure upon boys."

Fearing lest he might say that which would betray somewhat of our purpose in coming out on the lake, I added gloomily : —

"If my mother could know where we are thus imprisoned it would seem less hard; but she is like to be anxious concerning us when night falls, and we have not returned."

Then the dear lad, catching quickly at my reason for thus speaking, added : —

"It cannot be the English soldiers will deem it a crime that we were skating on the lake, and our release must soon come."

After that we fell silent, not daring to speak lest we reveal what should be kept a secret, and having at heart that fear of the future which quenched all desire for conversation.

As the moments passed and we were forced to remain inactive, crouching in the snow, exposed to the wind which came through every tiny crevice, our limbs became chilled, and I said to myself that we were like to freeze in these snug quarters where exercise was impossible save as one might swing his arms to and fro.

That gloom which I had assumed when we were first thrust into the pen now took possession of me in earnest, and again did I reproach myself with having allowed the headstrong Alec to go on when I knew we were in danger.

Then came that which caused us for the time to forget our private troubles.

A group of soldiers inside the hut which joined our prison, were talking so loudly that we could hear a goodly portion of the conversation, and Alec seized me by the hand to attract my attention when one of the men said impatiently: —

"There is no good reason why we are forced to halt here waiting for the remainder of the regiment. I venture to say that the Yankee settlement can be captured with threescore of men."

There was no need any one should tell us of what settlement they were speaking. If I had not suspected before, it would have been plain to me now, that this detachment had encamped here to make ready for an attack upon Presque Isle.

After a moment's silence another voice asked: —

"Does any one know when we are like to move?" and to this, reply was made by the man who had first spoken, so I judged: —

"When we number four hundred, I have heard it said."

"And how long are we to wait for the remainder of the detachment? Three days seem like a month, when one is tied up here, half frozen."

"There is no reason why the attack could not have been made two days ago," the first speaker replied. "I am told that those who should join us were halted at Port Ryers, but it is possible they may be here at any moment."

"There is nothing to delay us an hour after they come."

Then the men began speculating upon the possible defence which might be made by our people at Presque Isle, Alec and I listening intently for that which would give us further hint as to the proposed movement.

It appeared to be the belief of the men that our settlement would offer but little resistance, and I was surprised to know how well informed they were concerning the condition of affairs.

I question if my father could have told them more regarding the vessels on the stocks, or the length of time which might be required to finish them. It was evident beyond a question that in Presque Isle some one who had been trusted with all the details — perhaps one in authority — was playing the traitor.

During fully an hour these men talked of that which they counted to do, treating the matter as if the capture of Presque Isle was but a trifling task; and we — Alec and I — grew alternately hot and cold, as we realized what valuable information it would be possible to give were we at liberty.

Not until nightfall was any attention paid us, and then the door of the pen was opened, that a soldier might thrust in two small squares of corn-bread.

"The snow will serve instead of water," he said, with a leer; and then we were alone once more.

Until this time neither of us had spoken; each was so intent upon forming some plan of escape that he had no desire to talk of aught else.

When the scanty rations had been left us, and it was understood, from what the soldier said, that we were to remain there until morning, I could keep silent no longer.

"We will get out of this at any hazard!" I whispered to Alec. "It is certain an attack will soon be made upon the settlement for the purpose of destroying the half-finished vessels, and information must be carried even at the expense of our lives."

"I grant you that, Dicky Dobbins, and am willing to venture on any chance, however small; but first you shall tell me in what way we may set about carrying the information."

The question I could not answer, and he knew it full well even as he spoke.

The one thing in our favor, as it seemed to me,

was the fact that the Britishers had not taken away the skates. When we removed them, according to orders, I was not minded to leave behind what had cost me two dollars in lawful money and twelve muskrat pelts, therefore slung them over my shoulder.

Now if we could but escape from this pen, with five minutes, or even half that time, the start, there was no question in my mind but we might get off scot-free.

How to get out? That was the question I could not answer, and thus far Alec seemed to be equally in the dark.

The men in the hut adjoining our prison no longer talked sufficiently loud for us to hear, or when they did, there were so many speaking at the same time that we could not make out clearly the subject of the conversation.

The snow was still falling; but the air was rapidly growing colder, and I had little question that the storm would soon cease, for the temperature must have been several degrees below zero.

To remain in this place, every corner of which was searched out by the wind, would have been to freeze, and we ran to and fro as best we might, thrashing our arms together with such a noise that some one in the hut cried with a laugh : —

"The Yankee cubs won't be idle this night, that I'll venture to say;" and another, who may have had boys of his own at home, added:—

"It is barbarous to leave them there without so much as a blanket. If the shed was filled with snow, into which they might burrow, it would not be so bad."

"A bit of chill won't do them any harm, and in case they get home again it will serve to show the braggarts there what awaits them if they persist in believing it possible to prevent Britain from ruling the sea, or the land either, for that matter."

"We may make as much noise as pleases us, and those fellows will think only that we are trying to keep warm," Alec whispered.

"Well!" I replied, not understanding for the moment what he meant. "How much of satisfaction will you find in making a noise?"

"This much," the lad replied; and from that moment I understood that, despite the lack of years, he was my superior in such knowledge as became one who would be a soldier: "Instead of walking idly to and fro, what prevents us from spending our strength in trying to dislodge some of these logs?"

There was nothing to prevent it, as I admitted to myself; but how might we set about it?

Work of any kind would be welcome, yet it was

necessary young Perry show me how it might be begun.

And that he did, after looking about for a moment, feeling of the joints in each corner where the timbers were simply laid one upon another, and only slightly dovetailed together.

"The uppermost one should be pushed aside easiest," he said at length, "for no more than the weight of the roof rests upon it."

"Yet you must have something as a lever with which to work."

"I will use my shoulder, if it so be you can hold me on your back."

"That I will do, and for so long a time as you wish," I replied, with but little faith that he might succeed in his purpose.

It was true nothing save the weight of the roof rested upon these uppermost logs; but this was formed of green saplings, which, when taken as a whole, would prove a burden far too heavy for both of us, even though we could come at it handily, so I said to myself.

However, there was no harm in trying; and so much good would come of it that even in the failure we should be gaining needed exercise to keep us warm.

Crouching as one does who plays at leap-frog, I

rested my hands upon the logs forming the outer side of the pen, to hold myself steady, and Alec stood upon my back.

In this position he was forced to bend nearly double, and I saw at once that could I hold him up when he straightened his body, something must perforce give way.

"Are you ready?" he asked in a whisper, and I, mentally bracing myself for the effort, replied: —

"Do your best; but quickly, lest I fail to hold this position."

Alec Perry is a slightly built lad, and to look at him one would say his strength was hardly more than that of a woman, yet I soon found that it was far in excess of what his frame indicated.

For an instant it seemed as if the weight of a ton was pressing upon my bent back, and then I heard a dull, muffled sound, as if some heavy body had fallen into the snow on the outside.

The strain upon me was lessened wonderfully, and my heart leaped with joy and gratitude as the dear boy whispered excitedly: —

"We have thrown off the top log, Dicky Dobbins, and unless there be a sentinel outside who has heard the timber fall, we shall be free from this pen as soon as you are minded to make the venture."

He leaped down from my back, and, grasping both his hands to show my gratitude for his gallant and wondrous effort, for it was wondrous in view of his slight body, I replied:—

"We'll count thirty, Alec, and if by that time no alarm is given, it is for us to make good an escape, taking the chances of losing our way in the driving snow upon the ice, rather than remain here; for now has come the time when we may save Presque Isle from falling into the hands of the enemy."

CHAPTER III.

THE ESCAPE.

HOW it may have been with Alec Perry while we stood inside that pen, listening eagerly, and yet fearing lest we might hear something, I know not. As for myself, it was as if the blood in my veins was at boiling point, and I could hardly breathe because of the sense of suffocation which had come upon me.

At first I began to count as rapidly as it was possible to speak the figures in my thoughts, and then came the knowledge that by hastening the time ever so little I might be destroying our chances for escape.

In case the fall of the timber had been heard, and one of the soldiers came out to learn the cause of the noise, it was possible he would fail to observe what had been done, for the snow was so light that the log must be concealed from view in its frosty bed.

I say again, it was possible, even probable, that one or more of the Britishers might come out and yet fail to detect what we had done; but if Alec and I should begin the attempt a few moments too soon, all would be lost. Better waste half the night than try to gain sixty seconds of time, and in the doing cut ourselves off from all hope of gaining liberty.

Similar thoughts must have been in my comrade's mind; for when I had counted up to thirty, and then waited ten seconds to give fair measure, he clutched my arm as if advising that we remain yet a little longer.

And so we did, standing there hand in hand, looking toward the narrow aperture through which lay home and freedom.

While we thus hesitated there came into my mind the fear that after we gained the outside some of the more kindly hearted Britishers would enter the prison-pen in order to bring us coverings, lest we freeze to death; and I literally shivered with dread, fearing so much of charity might be bestowed upon us.

Then, when we had waited fully two minutes, I could restrain my impatience and my nervousness no longer.

Surely the very beating of my heart would betray us unless flight was begun at once.

I dared not so much as whisper, so great was the fear of discovery upon me, and pressing Alec's hand yet more vigorously, I pointed to the aperture.

He, understanding the gesture, motioned for me to go ahead; but that I would not do, and rather than play so cowardly a part as to seek my own safety first, I ventured upon speech: —

"You shall lead the way, Alec, lad," I whispered, my voice trembling despite every effort to render it steady; "and if it so be that when you have gained the outside the Britishers enter here, I beseech you to strain every muscle in the attempt to escape, regardless of what they may be doing to me."

"I will never leave a comrade alone in danger," he said stoutly; and for a moment it seemed as if we should come to a quarrel then and there, while halting 'twixt liberty and imprisonment.

"You must leave me, should the flight be discovered before I am out of here," I said earnestly, gripping his arm so hard that twenty-four hours later I saw the imprints of my fingers upon the flesh where the blood had settled. "It is neither your life nor mine that is to be considered now, but the safety of Presque Isle; and I charge you, dear lad, make your way to the settlement without loss of time, once you are free. I pledge myself to do the same, leaving you wherever it may be that we are halted by the enemy, in order to save the village and the vessels, upon which so much of our country's safety depends."

Now he understood what I would have him bear well in mind, and whispered : —

"One or the other of us must live to reach the village; but I pray earnestly, Dicky, that if either falls, it be me."

This sort of a conversation was not calculated to make a timorous fellow overly bold, and I realized at once that an end must be put to it, else we might become so faint-hearted as to retreat even before the advance was begun.

Therefore, clasping him by the legs, I lifted him straight up until his head and shoulders were through the aperture; and then, pushing at his feet, I literally forced him out of the pen.

Instantly this was done I reproached myself for having been so hasty, fearing lest he, like the log, might fall, failing to find support on the sides of the hut, and thus an alarm be given.

Alec Perry was not a lad to be guilty of a blunder, even though his comrade did his best toward forcing him into one; and in some way, I know not how, he contrived to drop from the top of the timbers as lightly as a cat.

Listening intently, I began to clamber up the wall, gripping my fingers into the crevices between the logs until the blood came from under my nails, and when

E

I was nearly at the top, the thought flashed upon me that we had left our skates behind.

They lay in one corner of the pen, and so great was our excitement, when the way of escape had been opened, that neither of us so much as thought of them.

Without skates we might as well remain where we were, for it would not be possible to walk across the lake in eight-and-forty hours.

I lowered myself down, losing the advantage I had gained at the expense of so much suffering, and thrust a pair of skates into each coat-pocket, after which the painful task of scrambling up the side of the pen was begun again.

It seemed to me of a verity that a full hour had been spent before I looked down from the top of the wall to see Alec making an effort to clamber back.

The time had dragged heavily with him also, and fearing lest some mishap had befallen me, he was returning, forgetful of the promises made to push forward at all hazards.

I heard plainly the sigh of relief which escaped his lips when he saw me, and in another instant I was lowering myself down on the outside.

Free, so far as concerned the walls of the pen!

Now the storm was little less than a blessing to

us, for the wind, howling and shrieking as it dashed the frosty particles against the walls of the huts, must have drowned any sound which we made while floundering through the snow.

A start of five minutes was all I had asked for, and this we surely would gain, unless it so chanced that a sentinel was stationed on the shore, in which case we stood every chance of being recaptured.

"It is necessary to go forward slowly, and by a devious way," Alec whispered. "It seems most likely some of the men are on guard, and it would be a sad blow to our hopes if we ran across them now."

"We must take the chances," I said, bolder grown since we were free from the pen. "To leave this path would be to flounder about in the snow or the bushes, where we must necessarily make so much noise that any sentinel, however dull, could not fail to hear us. There is no other course than to push ahead and trust to chances, Alec, lad. Besides, the danger in advance is less than that behind, and if we come upon a soldier near-by the edge of the ice, surely the two of us ought to be more than a match for him, half stupefied by the cold as any man must be who has remained long outside on this night."

There was no need for him to make answer. He stood ready to do whatsoever was needed, and I venture to say, however great the perils which menaced, he would not have flinched from braving them.

We went forward swiftly, yet making no noise that could be avoided, and when finally we were arrived at the shore of the lake no living thing could be seen.

"We are free, Dicky, lad! Free!" Alec cried, speaking so loudly that I covered his mouth with my hand, lest in his joyous excitement he work us the greatest mischief which could come upon two lads in our situation.

It can well be imagined that not a second was lost in fastening on our skates, and when we stood erect, shod with those thin plates of steel which would enable us to glide over the surface of the ice with the speed of a race-horse, it was with difficulty that I could repress a shout of triumph.

We two, who had never before known by experience the horrors of war and its usages, — we who had through carelessness allowed ourselves to be made prisoners, — were escaped without a scratch within a few hours of capture, and by escaping would be able to prevent Presque Isle from being taken by surprise.

When I bent my body in striking out on that long, swinging stride which had served me time and time before, I thought with exultation that that which had seemed the direst calamity that could come upon two lads, was, in fact, a blessing in disguise, as are many of the troubles which for the time bear us down in sorrow. Save for Alec Perry's foolhardiness in continuing on toward the Canadian shore, we would never have known of that gathering of soldiery at the North Foreland, and the people of Presque Isle, lulled into a sense of security, might have fallen easy victims to the first assault of the redcoats.

"It has been a good day's work, Alec, boy!" I said, when we were a mile or more from the shore, and escape was absolutely certain unless we lost our lives in the whirl of snow, for no man in that camp could overtake me on skates. "A good day's work, because we have scouted to a purpose, even though it was done ignorantly!"

The dear lad's mind went farther afield than mine, as I understood when he added quietly, yet with a certain ring of satisfaction in his tone: —

"So that we reach the village, Dicky, we have made a name for ourselves which shall be spoken in years to come, long after we are dead, for we will be known as the boys who saved Presque Isle and the beginnings of the American navy. It is what Oliver has been praying might be his good fortune, to come into some adventure which would give him an opportunity of making a name that should live in history; and God grant he succeed, for my brother is a hero, Dicky Dobbins, and some day he will prove it to those of the king's forces who come against him."

Fortunately at this moment I remembered that there must be an end to this self-glorification, and a speedy one, else were we likely to come to grief.

I had heard the bravest men in Presque Isle say that the one thing they feared the most was to be overtaken by a snow-storm while on that vast field of ice which imprisoned the waters of Lake Erie; for few there be who can walk or skate in a straight line amid the falling, whirling particles of snow.

We had come two miles, perhaps, from the shore by this time, and I caught Alec's arm, that he might take the better heed to my words, as I explained the dangers which were before us, begging that he put from his mind all else save the aim of moving forward as nearly in a straight line as might be.

"You shall go ahead, lad, keeping in advance so far as I am able to see you, and perhaps by this means it will be possible for me to know when you turn to the right or the left, as it is said one is ever inclined to do under such circumstances."

Perhaps if it had not been for our having foolishly run into the arms of the Britishers, Alec would have insisted that I was making a great cry when no danger threatened, because he seemed to think it a simple matter to go ahead in a straight line without anything to guide his movements; but now that the knowledge of his foolhardiness was sharp upon him he obeyed readily; and thus we set out on our thirty-mile journey in the darkness, our faces stung until they burned by the icy particles which were flung against them on the wings of the east wind.

Here again did that which seemed to be a danger and a discomfort prove a blessing. But for the wind we should have had nothing to give us the slightest idea of the direction in which Presque Isle lay. As it was, I could not say to a certainty that these furious blasts came from the east, because the direction might have changed since we were made prisoners; but I knew beyond a peradventure it had not swung around either to the north or the south, and, therefore, if our left cheeks were stung by the driving snow more bitterly than our right, we must be advancing somewhere near on the desired course.

During the first half-hour Alec went straight forward, and then, growing weary, perhaps, he would swerve to one side or the other, insisting, when I checked him, that it was I, rather than himself, who mistook the direction.

I am making this story of our escape from the North Foreland overly long, for it may be that what then seemed, and seems now, to me most thrilling, will be dry reading to others. Therefore it is best I come to a halt in this play of words, although it would be possible to fill page after page with what we thought, and said, and did during that long, painful night's journey; for, although we had set out, as nearly as we could judge, at about eight o'clock in the evening, the sun was two hours high in the heavens before we were come to Presque Isle, so nearly exhausted that Alec fell upon the shore, unable to move hand or foot, when we were arrived in front of my home.

Despite all our efforts we went so far astray as to strike the American shore near Indian Bend, full eighteen miles above the village, and arriving there during the hours of darkness, I was not able to say positively where we were; therefore it became necessary to wait until daylight.

This halt, while it refreshed us in a certain degree, allowed our limbs to stiffen until, when we arose to our feet again, it seemed almost impossible to advance one foot before the other.

But we were arrived at last, and could give the information which it was so necesssary our people should have; therefore was the work done well, even though death had come upon us after the story was told.

Strange as it may seem, we found it difficult to repeat that which we had learned. Every man was so engrossed with the work in hand that it appeared like a waste of time to listen to two lads who had been pleasuring on the Point, as was supposed; and we, fatigued beyond power of further movement, could not run from one to another insisting upon being heard.

But for the fact that Noah Brown chanced to pass near by where I was trying to induce one of the shipwrights to listen to me, it might have been a full hour before we gained the ear of any in authority.

Once I began to speak, however, and he realized from whence we had escaped, it can be fancied that no further entreaties on our part were necessary.

It was he who pleaded with us to tell more, and when the story of the adventure had been repeated twice over, an alarm was given which aroused every man, woman and child in Presque Isle.

What was done toward defending the place during the first four and twenty hours of excitement I know not, because, when our work had been accomplished,

Alec Perry and myself were given the needed opportunity to sleep, and until the morning after our arrival we realized nothing of what was passing around us.

It is now well known that the Britishers did not make an attack upon the village; but — and here I must go ahead of my story for a moment — we learned five months later, from a prisoner, that the expected reënforcements arrived twelve hours after our escape, and save for the fact that we had succeeded in giving them the slip, the assault would have been made without delay. The commandant decided, however, that the news which we carried regarding the assembling of the forces at that point would be sufficient to give an alarm, and concluded, with good cause, that it was no longer possible to take Presque Isle by surprise.

There was no lack of scouts on the lake from the day of our return until the ice broke up, and in the meanwhile my father had come back from Buffalo with a twelve-pound cannon, four chests of small arms, and a limited supply of ammunition.

It was a scanty store toward fitting out the vessels which were nearing completion; but it served to put us all in better spirits, because, with these much needed munitions, we could the better defend the bay.

Lest it should seem that I am vainglorious, the words which my father spoke to Alec and myself when he learned what we two had done shall not be set down here; but this much is necessary in order that what follows may be understood. He agreed, in the name of Captain Perry, that we lads should be allowed to enlist on whatsoever vessel pleased us; and promised also, in the name of Alec's brother, that a full report of our adventure be sent to the Government at Washington.

We still continued, so long as it was possible, to skate back and forth on the lake within half a dozen miles of the American shore, and perhaps I need not say that never again did Alec make any attempt at venturing farther across than seemed absolutely necessary.

When not thus employed we watched eagerly the building of the ships, and had much discussion between ourselves as to which one we should volunteer to serve on. For my part I was wholly at a loss to decide, until Alec settled the question by saying: —

"Where my brother is, there must be the hottest fighting, for I assure you he will seek out the enemy whether they be disposed to give battle or not; and when he returns from Pittsburg we shall know on which craft we are to sail."

Captain Perry came back on the 10th day of April. The ice was out of the lake, and the forces in the blockhouse at the entrance of Presque Isle Bay were redoubled, for now we had every reason to expect the British fleet.

Two weeks after his return the three gunboats were launched, and I dare venture to say not one person in Presque Isle, old or young, missed the spectacle.

It was a gala day in the village, and when we saw the little craft swinging at their cables just off the landing-place, there came to every one, I believe, to myself I know, an additional sense of security, although these vessels were as yet uncompleted, and without guns or ammunition.

The two brigs would be ready for leaving the ways in three weeks, it was said, and Alec and I looked forward to that day with the keenest interest, for Captain Perry had told us that upon one of these he should sail, while at the same time he ratified the promise made by my father.

We promised ourselves that nothing should prevent us from seeing these two craft, which both of us felt certain would make the bravest showing against the Britishers, leap into the water, and yet we failed of being present.

This is how it was:—

One week before the day set for the launching a message came from Commodore Chauncey, who was then at Buffalo, ordering Captain Perry to join him in a certain secret enterprise against the enemy.

Now Alec's brother was not minded to take two lads with him, and would have kept the matter secret, but that it came to us quite by accident.

Emboldened by the service already rendered, we decided that it was our right to accompany the expedition.

I need not repeat the arguments which we used to persuade the captain to receive us as volunteers. He objected to our proposition; first, because it was not expected he should bring any force with him, and secondly, because he must journey from Presque Isle to Buffalo in an open four-oared boat, which, in itself, was like to be a perilous undertaking at that season of the year.

Alec had a persuasive tongue, fortunately, as I then thought, and the result of our pleadings was that on the evening of the 23d of May, the day before the brigs were to be launched, we two lads embarked in what was hardly more than a skiff, manned by four oarsmen, with Captain Perry, exulting in the thought that now were we bearing men's parts in the war against the enemies of our country.

CHAPTER IV.

THE ATTACK.

WHAT might be the enterprise in which we were embarked on this 23d day of May, in the year 1813, neither Alec nor I could so much as guess, and we were not troubled because of our ignorance.

So that it was an attack upon the enemy, and a venture in which was somewhat of danger, we gave no heed.

As a matter of course we speculated upon it among ourselves, and, knowing that Captain Perry proposed to set out alone, we believed it was something in the nature of a reconnoissance, which in itself would have been comparatively trifling but for the fact that Alec's brother was making it, and he, we understood full well, would lead us as near to the Britishers as might be agreeable.

As I have said, it was evening when we set out from Presque Isle, embarking at the old French Fort, and before having sailed a distance of ten miles the boat was headed in for the shore.

To my mind there was good reason for this manœuvre. The wind was blowing from the north and
east a full half-gale, and it was such weather as
appeared too heavy for our small boat.

Immediately after we had rounded the point on
which was located the blockhouse, and were come out
into the lake, I believed the captain would decide that
it was dangerous in the extreme to make any attempt
at continuing the journey, and my relief was great
when the bow of the craft grated upon the sand.

"If this is to be the end of our travels we need
not have wasted so much breath in asking permission
to join the party," Alec whispered to me, laughingly,
but ere I could reply my father stepped out from
the bushes, pushed off the boat as he leaped into it
without speaking, and the voyage was resumed before
we had fully come to a halt.

Now it was we understood that some plan of operations had been decided upon beforehand, else would
Captain Perry and my father have held converse with
each other; but, instead, they sat in the stern-sheets
intent, so far as we could see, only upon the progress
which we might make by aid of oars.

Noting the expression on each man's face I grew
more serious in mind, understanding full well that they
had in view something of a grave nature, otherwise words

would have passed between them, whereas both held silent; while our boatmen fought against the angry waves of the lake as if some great reward awaited them in event of a successful ending of the voyage.

This much Alec saw as well as did I, for he whispered, after we had pushed out on the angry waters again, forcing our way against wind and wave half a mile or more, during which time no person in the boat had so much as spoken:—

"Where think you, Richard Dobbins, is to be the end of this adventure?" And I answered him, having in mind our captivity at Port Rowan:—

"It is like that we will head, so soon as the wind permits, for some point on the Canadian shore. Perhaps neither your brother nor my father firmly believes all we told them regarding the gathering of Britishers, and are now come to make a reconnoissance, since the ice is broken up and it is possible for troops to cross the lake."

It would have been as well had we held our peace, for neither Alec nor I guessed at the meaning of this voyage, as was shown when the night grew older.

Instead of proceeding toward the Canadian shore, as would have been easier under all the circumstances, we hugged the land so far as was possible, steadily advancing within what might well be called the American boundaries, straight on toward Buffalo, and were it not for the fact of what followed after we were on the banks of the Niagara River, I would write much concerning the dangers of that night voyage, when not only once, but twenty times, were we in great peril of being overset by the angry waves.

However, because of what followed, this venture, which at the time seemed in the highest degree hazardous, came to appear as nothing, and must be passed over with but few words.

Therefore let me set it down that during every moment of all the long night we two lads believed our lives were near to being ended.

Every wave which buffeted our slight craft sent the water in over rail or stern, and brought her down so low that the water broke over us until we were forced to bail with all our might, else had we been swamped.

In such manner did the night pass, and when morning broke we were at Buffalo, neither Alec nor I understanding what purpose could have brought us there.

We had a fairly good idea, however, when, with such horses as could most readily be procured, we four — meaning Captain Perry, my father, Alec, and I — set out by land, riding during that day and part of

F

the next night until we were come to Lewiston, when we made a halt.

Then a council was held, in which we had no part, but I heard Captain Perry say to my father at the close of it:—

"You will ride back to Schlosser, and there make ready boats in which to transport laborers who will hasten the work upon our squadron at Presque Isle, if it so be we are successful in the venture."

Whereupon my father asked:—

"But if it so be that you fail in the enterprise?"

"To my mind there is no such possibility. Fort George must be taken within four and twenty hours after our arrival, and from that point we will detach as many men as are needed for the movement which we contemplate upon the lake."

Thus it was that Alec and I gained an inkling of the whole scheme.

Fort George, on the Canadian shore, just south of Newark, was to be attacked by our forces, most likely under command of Commodore Chauncey, and we lads, who burned to distinguish ourselves, would be given the opportunity within a few hours.

My father turned back agreeably to the commands he had received, and we three continued on until we arrived at the shore of Lake Ontario, near-by Fort

Niagara, off which was lying the American fleet, consisting of such vessels as the *Madison, Oneida, Lady of the Lake, Ontario*, and five or six others whose names shall appear as this narrative progresses.

It was a hearty reception with which we met when, having come to the shore, signals were made to our vessels in the offing, and a boat put out from the *Madison*, which for the time was flying Commodore Chauncey's flag.

Leaving our horses in the care of friendly-disposed people near at hand, we embarked in the commodore's barge, and on stepping aboard the *Madison*, Commodore Chauncey said, taking Captain Perry warmly by the hand : —

"No person on earth could be more welcome at this time than yourself."

It was as if these words had been spoken to us two lads personally, and immediately Alec and I were puffed up with pride, sharing for the moment all the honor which was given to the captain.

It was not with any idea of spinning out a yarn regarding the capture of Fort George that I first set myself down to this task, but rather to tell how Captain Oliver Perry won renown for himself on the waters of Lake Erie, and also to describe the slight share which we two lads had in the gaining of his glory.

Therefore it is that all which was done here near-about Lake Ontario shall be given in the fewest words possible to a fair understanding. So far as we two lads are concerned, it may well be passed over briefly, for although our intentions were good, and we had fancied the moment was come when we could play the part of men, Alec Perry and I were little more than spectators during this, the first of warfare I had ever witnessed.

But even to so skeleton-like a tale as this must be, some words of description are necessary, in order that what share Captain Perry had in the victory may thoroughly be understood.

The commander of the American forces was General Henry Dearborn, and of the American squadron, as I have before said, Commodore Isaac Chauncey.

Of our land force, fit for duty, there were said to be over four thousand, including the troops under command of Major-General Lewis in Fort Niagara. Our people had, in addition to the fort I have just named, what was known as the Salt Battery, opposite Fort George, and two other batteries between it and Fort Niagara.

General Dearborn was so sick at this time as to be unable to take any active part in the operations; but his chief of staff, Colonel Winfield Scott, represented him ably, and during an interview between the commodore and the general in command, it was decided that Captain Oliver Perry should have full charge of the task of landing the troops when the attack was begun.

Further preparations on our side consisted of building a large number of small boats at Five-Mile Meadow, and orders were sent for them to be brought around to Four-Mile Creek on the evening of the 26th of May, when an interview between our commanders was held. These skiffs were to be used, as a matter of course, in the landing of the troops.

So much for the American forces; now for the British.

There were nearabout the fort which Commodore Chauncey and General Dearborn counted on taking, English regulars to the number of eighteen hundred, under command of Brigadier-General John Vincent. In addition, there were three hundred and fifty militia and fifty Indians under Colonel Harvey.

It was said by our spies that the enemy's force extended on the right from Fort George to Brown's Point, and on the left to Four-Mile Creek and the Canadian side of the river; while in the rear of the fortifications a number of companies were stationed to support each other when required.

Besides Fort George, the Britishers had several

smaller works along the shore of the Niagara River and Lake Ontario. One twenty-four pound gun was set up about half a mile from Newark, and their principal battery was at the mouth of Two-Mile Creek.

All this Alec and I learned while we remained on board the *Madison*, awaiting some word from Captain Perry, who was in consultation with the leaders of the American forces.

The sailors, knowing my father full well by reputation, for he was said to be one of the most skilful navigators upon the lakes, were more than ready to talk with me; but before the summer was come to an end it was Alec Perry to whom they gave their confidences, rather than to the son of Daniel Dobbins.

It was only natural we two lads should believe, having come thus far, that we would be allowed to share in the battle which all knew must follow, because, in such strong position as was the enemy, he would not allow his fortifications to be taken from him without a spirited resistance; but we were soon made to understand that however valuable we believed our services might prove, they were not to be accepted.

When, on the evening of the 26th, the final arrangements were made for an attack upon the British fort, and the leaders of the expedition had come on board the *Madison*, General Dearborn accompanying them despite his illness, Alec's brother explained to us, in a tone which admitted of no discussion, what part we were to take in the action of the morrow.

"You will stay quietly aboard the *Madison*, and under no circumstances make any attempt at accompanying the troops when they land. I have allowed you lads to remain with me thus far; but with the promise to Captain Dobbins that you should have no further share in the attack, than that of spectators."

A bitter disappointment it was, indeed, to see our people prepared for a battle which we firmly believed would result in a victory for the Americans, and yet remain idly by while glory, and perhaps fame, was to be won.

Because Alec stood silent when his brother had thus spoken, I understood that it would be useless to make any effort at persuading the captain into recalling the command given, and swallowed my disappointment as best I might.

Therefore it is that I am all the more willing to pass ov: the capture of Fort George with the fewest possible words.

Late in the afternoon the boats, which I have said had been built at Five-Mile Meadow, were pulled around to Four-Mile Creek, and this work brought on a general fire between the forts and batteries in the immediate vicinity; but, save for the destruction of several houses along the river bank, no injury was inflicted on either side.

From sunset until midnight the heavy artillery and a portion of the troops were embarked on the *Madison*, the *Oneida*, and the *Lady of the Lake*, while the remainder of the force, including the horses, were taken on board the newly constructed boats.

It can well be supposed that no heed was given to sleep after the work of embarkation had been concluded; all awaited the signal for the advance, knowing it must speedily come.

It was near to daybreak when our squadron got under way, and Alec and I stood on the after part of the *Madison* vainly trying to see, in the darkness and the fog, what was being done.

We could hear on every hand the murmur of voices, the creaking of oars in rowlocks, the neighing of horses, and the flapping of sails; but could see nothing.

It gave one a most singular sensation to be shut in by the dense, gray vapor, and yet to know from the various noises that on all sides were men making ready to take the lives of others, or to sacrifice their own.

The officers of the expedition, and among them as

a matter of course was Captain Perry, remained by themselves, as was proper, and we two lads would have given much just then could we have had speech with Alec's brother, in order that he might explain certain movements which to us were mystifying.

Then, suddenly, as it were, the heavy mist lifted and the sun shone out clear and warm, lighting up the waters which were cove.ed here, there, and everywhere, seemingly as far as the eye could reach, with vessels and small boats, all laden with men and implements of warfare.

It was a sight such as few lads could ever have the privilege of witnessing, and for a time I believed there was nothing so grand or so noble as war.

With the rising of the fog the wind freshened, and the vessels of the fleet advanced according to the programme mapped out.

The schooners *Julia* and *Growler* took up position at the mouth of the river, engaging the battery near the lighthouse where it was intended to land a portion of the troops. A short distance away toward the north, the *Ontario* came about to command the same position.

The *Governor Tompkins* and the *Conquest* were moored near Two-Mile Creek in front of a small battery where the remainder of our men were to be set ashore. Coming up with these two schooners were the *Hamilton*, the *Asp*, and the *Scourge*, and before they were all in such position as had been previously agreed upon, the batteries on both sides of the river opened fire.

The first notes of the battle were being sounded.

Now had come the time for Alec's brother to display that courage which afterward won for him so great a name, and we two lads gave more heed to his movements than to all else beside.

The *Governor Tompkins* and the *Conquest* immediately opened fire on the battery they were ordered to silence, and the wind, which was momentarily increasing in force, swept away the smoke until we from the deck of the *Madison* could see all that took place.

It seemed to me as if no more than five minutes elapsed before the Britishers fled from their earthworks, and Captain Perry had leaped overboard from the foremost of the fleet of boats, wading to the shore, with the men close behind him like a party of schoolboys at play.

Colonel Scott was not far in the rear of Alec's brother, and these two brave men led the way up the embankment, despite the rapid musketry firing which was poured upon them from Britishers concealed in the thicket hard by.

"CAPTAIN PERRY HAD LEAPED OVERBOARD FROM THE FOREMOST OF THE
FLEET OF BOATS."

Even to Alec and I, who were ignorant regarding what is called the "art" of warfare, it seemed as if the schooners were not discharging their guns as rapidly as possible, while the Britishers ashore were pouring a hot fire into our men.

Without being really conscious of the fact, we set up a shout of exultation when we saw Captain Perry push off in a boat alone, regardless of the bullets which were falling into the water in every direction, and row toward the nearest schooner.

In less than three minutes from the time he stepped on board the vessel we knew for what purpose he had gone. The schooner's guns were served much more rapidly than before, and then it was that the captain went ashore again to take his full share in the conflict which was raging, for now indeed was the battle on.

Because of the smoke, we two lads could not see plainly all that was done; but General Dearborn, with a glass at his eyes, followed the action closely, and by the words which fell from his lips at frequent intervals we understood that our men were more than holding their own.

It is said that the battle lasted only about twenty minutes; but I could equally well have believed it was half that time, or even so long as three hours, so wrought up by excitement was I.

However, we knew full well when the shouts from the shore, and the rapid forward movements of our men, told that the victory had been won, — that Fort George was ours, — and even though we two lads had had no share in the fighting, we raised our voices as loudly in triumph as did those whose brave deeds had vanquished the foe.

As we afterward learned, our loss in the battle was about forty killed and an hundred wounded; while of the British fifty-one were killed and eight hundred and twelve regulars and militiamen either wounded, missing, or made prisoners.

Alec and I, still forced to remain aboard the *Madison* because of the orders given by Captain Perry, knew little of what was being done until far into the night, when we heard that the British commander, General Vincent, was in full retreat; that all the enemy's fortifications on the Niagara River were abandoned because of the victory just won.

It was near to daybreak next morning when Captain Perry came on board the flag-ship and told us that we were to set out on the return to Presque Isle without delay.

And so we did, beginning the journey within half an hour after sunrise, despite the fact that Alec's brother had not slept for eight and forty hours, making all speed down the river as if our army had been defeated, and we were fleeing in wild disorder before a victorious enemy.

We understood full well, however, why our return must be made with such great speed.

There were at the Black Rock Navy-Yard, above Buffalo, five vessels which had been prepared for warlike service, and peradventure we could arrive there before the British destroyed the place, these craft might be ladened with such material as we at Presque Isle stood most in need.

Even now, after so long a time has passed, it seems to me that I might profitably fill many pages with an account of our journey down the river, the halt at Black Rock Navy-Yard, the loading of those vessels built by Henry Eckford, and of the passage back to Presque Isle when, with a force of two hundred soldiers, as many sailors as could be hired, and all the oxen to be found in the vicinity, these craft, so sadly needed by our people, were towed, or tracked, along the shore of the lake.

There was much of interest which befell us on the way during this long and tedious journey, for we did not get the vessels loaded and into Buffalo until the 6th of June, nor sail from there until the 13th, when Captain Perry lay in his berth on board the *Caledo-*

nia sick with what appeared to be a fever, and it seemed to Alec and I as if, because of this illness, all which had been accomplished was set at naught, so far as concerned the getting under way of the fleet that had been begun by my father.

CHAPTER V.

THE BRITISH FLEET.

AS I have said, our little fleet sailed from Buffalo on the 13th of June, and on board the *Caledonia* Captain Perry lay sick with a fever.

Perhaps Alec and I were the only two who placed such great dependence upon the leader of this expedition. It may be that others, better informed concerning such matters, held to it that there were many who could fill the place to which Oliver Perry had been appointed; but in my mind his death meant the direst disaster — his sickness the deferring of all our hopes.

As a matter of course Alec and I were also embarked on the *Caledonia*, for we two played the part of nurses to the fever-stricken captain, and although as ignorant in matters of sickness as we were in the art of warfare, I dare venture to say the invalid never suffered for anything whatsoever that it was within our power to give him.

I was distressed in mind because of Captain Perry's

illness so as to give no heed to the fact that we were making our way toward Presque Isle at imminent danger of being captured by the enemy, although even the dullest member of the party could have said beyond a peradventure that the British had vessels in plenty on Lake Erie, and would most likely be on the lookout for those who were returning from the successful attack upon Fort George.

One thing that both of us lads were alive to, however, was the slow progress our fleet was making.

The breeze was hardly more than strong enough to ruffle the surface of the waters, and during the first four-and-twenty hours we advanced only that number of miles, Captain Perry meanwhile eating his heart out with impatience because of the dull sailing, thereby giving us quite as severe a task as we could perform in keeping him below according to Dr. Parson's orders.

When we were thus come twenty-four miles in as many hours, and the little fleet of vessels and boats lay becalmed upon the mirror-like lake, a canoe, in which were two men, put out from the American shore, one of the boatmen paddling vigorously, while the other waved a small flag in such manner as gave us to understand that they were either fleeing from pursuit, or bringing important intelligence.

Becalmed as the *Caledonia* was, we could do no less than await the coming of these strangers, even had we been otherwise disposed; and when they were finally arrived on board we had ample food for reflection and fear.

The British squadron, under command of Captain Finnis, was even at that time searching for us, so the newcomers reported; within eight-and-forty hours they had passed over this same course, and in such force as boded ill for us should we chance to come upon them.

The squadron consisted, so we were told, of the ship *Queen Charlotte*, carrying seventeen guns; the schooner *Lady Prevost*, with thirteen guns; the brig *Hunter*, having ten guns; the schooner *Little Belt*, mounting three guns, and the *Chippewa*, of one gun.

Our little fleet consisted of the brig *Caledonia*, mounting two small guns (the same craft which had been captured on the ninth of October under the guns of Fort Erie by the expedition in command of Lieutenant Elliott); the schooner *Somers*, which carried one long twenty-four-pounder; the schooner *Ariel*, with one long eighteen-pounder; the schooner *Ohio*, with one long twenty-four-pounder, and the sloop *Contractor*,[1] with one long eighteen-pounder, to say nothing of the small boats.

[1] Afterward renamed the *Trippe*.

G

Taking all our armament into account, we could add to such a number of guns as I have mentioned, perhaps two hundred muskets, therefore it behooved us to keep out of the way if possible.

When those who brought the disagreeable intelligence came on board the *Caledonia*, Captain Perry was lying in his berth; Dr. Parsons had just given him a most bitter potion, and Alec and I stood by with fans, for the heat in the close cabin was almost unbearable.

I watched the young captain closely, expecting to see some show of fear when he learned in what force the enemy had mustered; but it was as if that which to nearly every one was most unwelcome intelligence, only served to animate him.

Despite the doctor's angry protest and Alec's pleading, the captain leaped to his feet, and of a verity I believe that the information brought by the strangers did more toward breaking up the fever which had held him captive, than any of the drugs Dr. Parsons administered.

From that moment it was as if he had never been ill, and without delay every precaution was made for defence, much as though he counted on forcing a battle with the enemy should we come within range, instead of running away, as would have been the proper manœuvre.

Such weapons as we had were distributed among those on the small boats as well as the vessels, and from that time until we were come safely within the sheltering arms of Presque Isle bay each man remained on the alert, even the most cowardly excited to bravery by the bold spirit which our young captain displayed.

I might go on at great length, describing how the entire force was divided into two watches so that the Britishers might not take us by surprise; telling of this or that alarm which caused us to believe a battle to be near at hand, and sent the blood bounding within my veins until I trembled with fear lest the fever of excitement should be that of cowardice; but where there is so much to be related, such incidents as then seemed of importance, but were afterward shown to be trifling, have no place in the tale that has for one of its characters such a man as Captain Perry.

We entered Presque Isle bay on the 19th of June at three o'clock in the afternoon, and the *Caledonia*, which was hove to outside until every other craft crossed the bar, had no sooner gained the shelter of the land than the British squadron arrived in sight.

Now, indeed, did Alec and I witness the preparations for a battle. The small boats were immediately ordered inshore with the tidings, and from the easternmost battery to the blockhouse farthest west on the mainland, the note of alarm was sounded.

Our little fleet was drawn up at the entrance of the bay; the gunboats and brigs, although not yet completed, were moored near at hand, but inside our line of battle, that they might be used as floating batteries for militiamen, and when the sun went down I question if there was an American within sight or sound of these preparations who did not believe the British would make an attack before morning.

And yet all of us were happily disappointed, for while we nerved ourselves for the struggle which it seemed certain must come, the most sanguine among us — and I believe I am warranted in putting among them Captain Perry himself — could not have believed we might come out victorious in a struggle with such a squadron as was under command of Captain Finnis.

However, we gave the Britishers every opportunity, determined to make as brave a fight as might be, and knowing full well that when we were beaten it would not be because we lacked in pluck.

This much I set down as information — not in the spirit of boasting, and in no wise to praise myself, for throughout it all I felt timorous when Alec was most brave, and near to being cowardly when Captain

Oliver was panting to meet the enemy. It is regarding the inhabitants of Presque Isle, who stood ready to defend the town, that I speak when writing of stout-heartedness, and not of myself.

Well, the king's squadron cruised off and on the entrance of the bay from nearabout three o'clock in the afternoon until the next morning at ten, and then, instead of standing boldly in when, after a few hard knocks, they might have gotten the best of our little force and destroyed what was the beginning of a navy, they turned about, beating as plain a retreat as if we had gone out to drive them away.

Alec was disappointed, because he believed his brother had lost an opportunity of distinguishing himself, while I rejoiced, knowing that for the time being at least we avoided an encounter which could have had but one ending.

War, when one looks at it from a distance, may appear very fine; but I assure whoever shall chance to read these lines that it wears a different aspect when one is forced to take a part in it. There is more glory seen from afar than at short range, and so much regarding fighting I can say from my own experience.

The unfinished gunboats and brigs were sent back to the shipyards when it was known beyond peradventure that the enemy had turned tail, and the *Caledonia*, and two or three others which had been brought down from Black Rock Navy-Yard, remained on guard at the entrance of the bay.

The brave Captain Finnis, with a force fully three times as large as ours, had decided that it might be neither healthy nor agreeable for him to stir up so much of the American eagle as was represented by our little force at Presque Isle.

Then the *Caledonia* also came inside, being moored just opposite the town, and for the first time since we had set out with Captain Perry did I have an opportunity of speaking with my mother.

She, good soul, was as pleased at seeing me as I at being with her, and during fully two hours I realized as never did a boy before how much of comfort there is to be found at home.

Alec shared in my pleasure to a certain degree, and I believe he hoped, as did I, that we might remain many days ashore, for our expedition to Fort George had not brought us overly much of happiness, and surely none of glory.

Then, when it seemed that my sense of enjoyment was keenest, when the pleasure of being at home was at its height, the second mate of the schooner *Ariel* presented himself at the door of my father's house, and after stiffly saluting my mother, who had answered his summons, said : —

"Captain Dobbins' compliments, and he asks that you will send to him immediately the two young gentlemen. They have been detailed for special service."

Saluting again, the sailor returned to the shore, and I can answer that two of the three in the house at that time were made heavy hearted because of his message.

Whatever Alec may have thought, I know not; he professed to be well pleased at the idea of active service, for it could readily be understood that such was the meaning, for us, of the summons.

My mother, dear soul, struggling hard to prevent any sign of disappointment from displaying itself on her face, bustled around as if her feelings might be kept in check by employment. She made up a package of provisions, knowing that however great was the grief in our hearts the time must come when such as she could provide would be most acceptable; and I, not minded that Alec might see any show of weakness in me, refrained from the loving embrace which no lad should be ashamed to bestow upon his mother.

Then I led the way out of the house with no more than a wave of my hand in token of adieu, and ten minutes later we were standing on the *Ariel's* deck.

I had noticed a trim-looking craft, which I took for

a pleasure boat, lying alongside when we came aboard; but gave no other heed to it at the moment, save as I said to myself that we had visitors from along the lake front, who, perchance, had brought such information as led to the summons sent Alec and I.

"Captain Perry is in his cabin on the *Caledonia*, and the doctor's orders are that he be not disturbed, because the fever is showing itself once more," my father said gravely, and I knew from the expression on his face, as well as his manner of speaking, that he had something of a serious import to impart. "It is reported that the British are concentrating at Long Point, and I would have you two lads make the attempt at discovering if such be true. The work can more safely be done by boys than men. The small craft which lays alongside is provisioned for a short cruise, and in her you should be able to reconnoitre the Canadian shore without much risk of being captured."

It was not for me to question the command, even though given by my father, and yet so great was the surprise which came with his words that I lost sight entirely of what might be military duty.

"Is our fleet to remain idle here in the bay?" I asked, and the same question was written on Alec's face, although he had more good sense than to put it into words.

"Even though all the vessels were ready we could not sail without men. The soldiers who came up with us from Buffalo as a guard have been ordered back, and, as you well know, we have no more of a force at present than is sufficient to handle one of the brigs."

"Then of what avail was it to build a fleet here at Presque Isle?" I asked stupidly.

"We have had reason to expect reënforcements long before this; but at present the only move that can be made is to acquaint ourselves with what the enemy may be doing. Go on board the small boat, and, without running heedlessly into danger, gain all the information that may be possible, returning here only when you have news of importance to impart."

It was easy to see that the subject was a sore one with him, and I needed not much experience in such matters to understand that a man like my father would feel most bitterly the necessity of remaining idle while the enemy was within striking distance.

As he felt, so probably did Captain Perry, and Alec and I came to know later how these two brave men chafed, being held prisoners within the harbor, as it were, when a few miles away was an opportunity, not only to win renown for themselves, but to strike a blow in aid of their country.

I understood only a portion of this at the time; but

that little was enough to prevent me from saying anything more, and obeying Alec's gestures I turned about
to go over the rail into the small boat.

My father stopped me with a touch on the shoulder,
and as I turned, he said, looking affectionately into my
eyes: —

"Be careful, Richard. Go so far as an American
should, regarding not your own life when there is need
that it should be sacrificed; but having a heed to your
steps when nothing can be accomplished by venturing."

Then he wheeled about as if not minded to see us
depart, and Alec and I went over the *Ariel's* rail
into as trim a pleasure boat as I had ever seen.

She was perhaps eighteen feet long, with a sort of
cuddy aft where one might be sheltered in case of a
storm, and rigged in sloop fashion, carrying a single
jib and mainsail.

There was a light breeze from the south, and when
we, having cast off the painter, hoisted the canvas, the
little craft slipped away from the schooner's side as
if under the influence of a full gale of wind.

Not until we were well out into the lake did either
of us lads make any comment upon this mission with
which we had been intrusted, and perhaps we held
silent the longer because it had come to us so sud-

denly that we were embarked in the enterprise before fully realizing it had been begun.

After we were two or three miles from the shore my thoughts went back to that winter afternoon when, having come on much the same course across the ice, we ran into the enemy's hands, and all the details of that disagreeable venture came into my mind. The unpleasant memories must have shown themselves in my face, for Alec, who was sitting well forward while I minded the helm, said banteringly : —

"Now that you are put in command of a vessel, the weight of responsibility seems to bow you down."

"It does indeed," I replied, surprising him by turning that which he counted should be a jest into a serious remark. "Not that I think my responsibility any greater than yours; but to my mind we are set out on a venture wherein is far more of danger than we have yet encountered."

"And you draw a long mouth because we may, perchance, run our heads into some peril?" he asked reproachfully.

"It is not that which troubles me so greatly, Alec Perry, as you should know full well by this time, having been comrades with me these three months. My gloomy thoughts are not brought about by fear of what may come to us; but because of the condition of affairs, as has just been represented to us."

"And are you but this moment come to realize that we have built vessels, and yet have no force to man them? Has it just dawned upon you that the British can enter Presque Isle with but little opposition?"

"I had believed sailors would be sent as soon as needed," I replied, looking at him in surprise, for there was a certain bitterness in his tone which gave me to understand he had been turning the unpleasant thought in his mind for many a day. "How long is it since you have had an understanding of the situation?"

"When we lay at the Black Rock Navy-Yard I half surprised, half forced Oliver into a confession that he was sorely disappointed because no heed had been given his request for men."

"And said nothing to me?"

"I promised him I would hold my peace until the fact should be apparent to all."

"Why such secrecy?"

"He feared any word from himself or me might be misconstrued, and that the people would think we gave ourselves up to complaint, instead of trying to make the best of what was a sorry affair. Now, since your father has spoken, there is no reason why I should longer hold my peace."

Then the lad repeated all his brother had said to him, and I, who should from my own observation have understood long since the true situation, now for the first time got an inkling of the defenceless position in which was Presque Isle.

I learned that Captain Perry had been ordered again and again by the officials at Washington to make some demonstration against the enemy, although it was well known that he had no more than sufficient force to man one of the brigs.

I had previously believed many of our recruits were in the hospital, but until now was not aware a full fifth of them were unfit for duty, and that even though it was possible the *Caledonia* alone might deal some disastrous blow to the British, she could not be sent out in proper trim.

Should Captain Finnis visit the bay with his cruising squadron on this day, he would encounter but little opposition, and the town, as well as our nearly completed fleet, would be at his mercy.

We talked long regarding the situation, Alec and I, wondering why the officials at Washington should neglect us so entirely — why Captain Perry had been sent up from Newport to take charge of a force which had no existence ; but could hit upon nothing by way of a solution to what seemed like a mystery.

It was a sorry beginning to a voyage full of dangers, as ours must necessarily be, and at the time it seemed that by declaring war against the Britishers the people of the United States had compassed their own destruction.

So despondent had we two lads become by this time that little heed was given to anything around, although liberty and perhaps life itself depended upon our vigilance. It was as if we were sailing the boat only for our own pleasure, regardless of where the wind might bear us, and we failed to keep even an ordinary lookout.

Therefore it was that both Alec and I were startled —almost frightened —when suddenly there came as if from out of the water, the cry:—

"Boat ahoy!"

For an instant I stared at Alec stupidly, and then, realizing how careless we had been, I sprang to my feet, looking wildly about.

The cry was repeated, and by bending outboard ever so slightly I saw just ahead of us, where we must have run her down had we held the course two or three minutes longer, a small boat, better known to us in Presque Isle by the name of bateau — a craft half canoe, half skiff, such as the Canadians use on swiftly running water — and in her, but making no effort to paddle out of the way, was a lad of about my own age, who waved his arms frantically to attract our attention.

I pulled the tiller up so that we might pass him on the starboard side, and as our boat swung off I understood why he had remained idle until we were near to running him down.

In the bateau was not so much as a paddle. The lad was powerless to direct her movements, and I stared at him stupidly in amazement, wondering how it chanced that he should thus be drifting so far from land at the mercy of wind and wave.

CHAPTER VI.

LEON MARCHAND.

WHILE Alec and I gazed at the frightened-looking occupant of the bateau, our craft was gliding swiftly by, and the lad, believing we intended to leave him in his plight, shrieked wildly : —

"In the name of mercy take me aboard your boat! Do not desert me!"

From his manner of speaking I understood that he was what we round about Presque Isle call a French-Canadian, and as such it was reasonable to suppose he had no very great love for the British.

However, whether he had been a friend or foe it was not my purpose to leave him, for should the wind increase to a gale he would be in great danger, while if it fell calm the lad was like to die from thirst or hunger.

Our craft was not to be brought around in an instant, and the boy, who could have known but little of seamanship, believing we intended to run away from him, redoubled his cries for help.

"Have patience until we can lay you alongside," Alec shouted with no little tinge of anger in his tones, for it seemed childish that this fellow should suppose we could bring the eighteen-foot boat up into the wind as we pleased.

The lad was so thoroughly frightened that he seemingly failed to understand anything we said to him; but continued to shriek imploringly, while we manœuvred our boat as best we might in a wind so strong that it was necessary to run off for a mile or more before we could stand back toward him.

"He is even more than an ordinary coward!" Alec exclaimed, as the boy's cries came to us, while, if he had had his wits about him, he must have seen that we were doing all in our power to get alongside the bateau.

"It is not strange he shows signs of fear," I said, feeling wondrous kind toward him just then because of the timorousness which had been in my heart a few moments previous. "He who is adrift on the lake without means of even so much as steering his boat, has a hard lookout ahead of him."

"He might at least hold his peace, knowing what we are trying to do."

"It may be he is no sailor, and fails to understand why it is necessary we run so far down before putting

H

back," I replied; and from that moment Alec held his peace, although I understood full well by the expression on his face that the lad's continued appeals for help annoyed him greatly.

Well, to make a long story short, we laid him alongside in due time, and once our craft rubbed against the gunwale of the boat, he leaped aboard in frantic haste, as if believing every second was precious.

As a matter of course his light craft, propelled by the impetus which he gave her in jumping, swung off beyond our reach, and, much as I pitied the lad, it was impossible to prevent an exclamation of impatience because of his carelessness.

The boat was worth more dollars than I had ever been possessed of at one time, and to send her adrift thus recklessly was an extravagance such as I could not countenance.

"What are you about?" Alec asked, when I swung the boat around in order to come at the skiff.

"I am counting on picking up the bateau. There is no reason why she should be allowed to go adrift when we may as well tow her into Presque Isle. A craft like that won't hold our boat back a half a mile in an hour."

"You didn't set out for the purpose of making a dollar," Alec said, speaking more sharply than I had ever heard him. "We have no right to waste time, and that same I would say even though yonder skiff was worth ten times what she will fetch."

Involuntarily I allowed our boat to swing around into the wind once more, surprised as well as pained by his tone, and until we were on our course again I gave no heed to the passenger who had so unceremoniously come aboard.

Alec, understanding that he had spoken roughly, said in a soothing tone, such as no lad, however angry, could withstand: —

"It was not in my mind to say aught to offend, Dicky; but knowing how important it is that we perform our mission, any delay, however slight, seems criminal."

My anger fled on the instant, and after one regretful glance at the bateau now so far astern, I held out my hand to him in token that I bore no ill-will, after which, following the direction of his gaze, I looked at the stranger.

He was a slight, weakly lad, with eyes such as would cause one to trust in him; but a certain timid way that told he had been delicately reared — a lad toward whom one's sympathy went out before he asked it.

"How came you adrift in a bateau?" and Alec looked at him searchingly as he spoke.

"The English soldiers, who last night sailed toward the American shore, left me to drown or starve."

"Left you?" I repeated, not understanding the words. "Do you live on our side of the lake?"

"My home is on the North Foreland, or, as perhaps you call it, Long Point. I offended the soldiers, and they took me with them, counting, as I then believed, to leave me with the Americans. Instead of which I was, shortly before daylight, put into the boat and told to go my way."

"Then the Britishers were reconnoitring Presque Isle Bay?" Alec asked quickly.

"They went in that direction, as I understood from their words, to see what preparations were being made."

"Where did they come from?"

"From the North Foreland."

"How many are there?"

"More than a thousand; and it is said they will march across the United States even into the capital city, Washington."

Alec looked at me as if to say that in befriending this lad we had indeed found a prize, for before having sailed half-way across the lake there was come to us such information as must be valuable to those at Presque Isle, who were waiting in vain for reënforcements.

"How did it chance that they could find pleasure

in thus setting you in danger of death?" I asked, still so taken by the lad's pitiful face that I failed to realize how important was the information he gave us.

"I refused to show them where my mother had hidden our store of provisions, and they could have killed me before I would have led them to it, for once it was taken, my mother and my sister might starve on the North Foreland, and I was not minded to bring about their death."

I failed to understand all he meant by this; but it was evident that he had proven himself courageous in a certain sense, otherwise the Britishers would not have dealt so hardly with him.

It is needless for me to set down here word for word the conversation which was held between us three as we continued on our course, holding steadily for Long Point, where he had said the enemy were yet in camp, because the story may be told in fewer words.

From the information given, neither Alec nor I had any doubt but that the Britishers were still encamped where we had found them on that certain day in March, and the movement against Presque Isle had been deferred, not abandoned.

I had no question but that he came from the same place where we were held prisoners, for by his story we understood that his mother lived not far from the extreme easterly point of land, where, as I knew full well, was a small farm under fairly good cultivation.

The British had been there more than three months, and twice during that time set out toward the American shore, but only to return. Why they failed to make an attack the lad could not say.

After he had given us all the information in his power, we asked his name.

"Leon Marchand," was the reply; "and my mother is the widow of that Captain Marchand who came hither from France eight years ago."

There was little in this statement to enlighten us; but I afterward came to understand why he spoke so proudly of his father, as will any lad who reads of what occurred nearabout Paris in the year 1804.

It can well be fancied that we looked upon this French lad as a friend, after once hearing his story, and that we trusted him fully, knowing he had little cause to feel kindly toward our enemies. In fact, so well convinced was I of his friendliness that, regardless of Alec's warning look, I explained why we were sailing across Lake Erie at a time when Americans had every reason to shun the Canadian shore.

"I shall help you to find out all you have come to learn," Leon said enthusiastically, having regained his cheerfulness immediately I confided in him. "Trust me to point out a safe harbor, and this night you may sleep at my mother's house."

There was a great question in my mind as to whether Alec and I were warranted in going ashore, for it seemed at the moment as if we had already learned that which should be told my father without delay, and I believed we ought to return at once.

"We will do as Leon suggests," Alec said, answering the question which he read in my eyes. "In order to accomplish our work we must know more. It is not enough that we go back and say there is yet an encampment of the enemy on Long Point."

"But we can discover no more by going ashore," I objected; and Leon, fearing lest it was in my mind to put about at once, cried imploringly : —

"Surely you will not take me with you? I can conduct you to a place where it will be easy to make a landing."

"You shall be left as near to your home as is safe for us," I replied, and immediately Alec added, as if his was the right to direct our movements : —

"We will sleep at your mother's home, Leon, and in payment for the rescue you shall show us during the night so much of the British encampment as we may wish to see."

"I am ready to do whatsoever you shall direct,"

the lad replied, and I made no protest, for suddenly, as it were, Alec Perry had taken upon himself the leadership. I had become no more than a follower who must obey his commands.

For the moment this sudden and seemingly unwarranted assumption of authority displeased me greatly, and then, remembering all that had taken place since we two met, I realized that he had the better head for such work as we were then engaged in.

Immediately I became only the helmsman, and from that hour Alec Perry was, in my mind, one who should be obeyed.

Leon gave us all possible information concerning the enemy's encampment, described the location of his mother's farm, and told of a cove near by where we might put in without great danger of being observed by the enemy, providing we did not land until after sunset.

Then it was Alec ordered the boat to be held on such a course as would keep us at a safe distance from the land until nightfall.

We broached the store of provisions which my mother had prepared for us; found a keg of water in the cuddy of the boat, and made as hearty a meal as if there was no such thing as war or soldiers in the land.

More than once as we neared the Canadian shore did we sight a sail; but with the breeze that was blowing, and the handy craft under us, it was not a difficult matter to give these strangers as wide a berth as suited our fancy.

Until half an hour before the close of day we stood off four or five miles from the land, taking good care, however, not to come within view of the sentinels who were likely posted nearabout the camp.

Then, in accordance with Alec's command, I hauled our light craft around for that portion of the shore pointed out by Leon, and we advanced toward the enemy's country as calmly as if going to meet a near and dear friend.

The night had fully come before we ran into a narrow cove, on the upper side of the North Foreland, where even in broad day we might have remained hidden from view of any who passed within an hundred yards, so dense and near to the water's edge was the forest which lined the shore.

Pulling the light boat as far into the thicket as was possible, we left her, and Leon led the way toward his home, having explained meanwhile that the British encampment was not less than a mile and a half away.

The reception which we met with from the Widow

Marchand was a warm one, as can well be imagined, and had we come for no other purpose than to restore her son, I should have felt that we were fully repaid for all the labor expended in his behalf.

She, as may well be fancied, had been in great distress of mind because of his absence, and now that he was with her once more, her anxiety to show gratitude was so great as to be most painful.

Alec, with a view to checking her efforts at displaying thankfulness, explained at considerable length how we had come upon him, and why he might do more for us than we had for him, whereat I could see plainly that the good woman was in much distress of mind.

She realized that Leon should do somewhat toward repaying us; but feared to have him venture within reach of those men who had shown to what length their cruelty could go.

"Your son has no need to do more than point out the location of the encampment, in case we decide to go there," I said, hastening to quiet her mind, and Leon interrupted by declaring positively that he should not leave us until we had accomplished our mission.

Well, we had a controversy there, Alec taking sides with me in the declaration that we would not lead the lad into further danger, and his mother, her gratitude outweighing her fears, insisting with him that it was his duty to do whatsoever lay in his power toward furthering our mission.

The result of it was that after partaking of a supper cooked in an outlandish fashion, although most palatable, we three lads set out to reconnoitre the British camp, I saying to myself meanwhile that it was not only a hazardous, but a foolish proceeding, for what could we hope to learn more than was known already?

The British were there in force, for Leon had good proof of such fact, and were threatening Presque Isle, which to my mind was as much as we needed to ascertain.

I did not venture to dissuade Alec from the reconnoissance, knowing full well that it would be useless, but believing we were venturing more recklessly into danger than when we had skated straight toward this same encampment three months before.

Leon led us by a roundabout way, skirting here along the shore, and again making a detour across the wooded lands until we were come to what was seemingly the rear of the camp, and here lay all the proof we needed.

So far as eye could see in the darkness, there appeared to be twice one thousand soldiers in the camp, and off the shore lay four vessels which I doubted not belonged to Captain Finnis's squadron, rendezvoused here ready to transport troops when the moment had come for the attack upon Presque Isle.

Leon, knowing full well all the paths through the woods, and the places where the sentinels were stationed, conducted us in safety from one point to another until I came to a halt, whispering to Alec: —

"There is no reason why we should continue this investigation any further. We already know as much as is necessary, and ought to be well on our way toward the American shore before day breaks."

"It was said that we should be absent two or three days, and I am not minded to leave here with no more information than has been gained," my comrade said stoutly, and in such a tone as told me that argument on my part would be useless.

"You will wait here to no further end than that we may be made prisoners," I replied hotly, and perhaps might have said what would have caused bad blood between us but that we were suddenly confronted by what seemed to me most imminent danger.

We were standing on one side of a broad path which ran, so Leon had declared, directly through the camp, when without warning a group of men appeared in the distance, coming directly toward us.

To have made any effort then at running away would have simply been to betray our whereabouts, for the rustling of the foliage must have told plainly where we were, and instinct prompted my companions as well as myself to step quietly back a few paces, where we might be screened by the leaves.

It was as if we had been led to the spot by some invisible power, for perhaps nowhere else could have been learned what we then heard.

The officers, for such we soon made out the strangers to be, were walking leisurely up the path in earnest conversation, as if strolling in the night simply to find relief from the heat; and soon we could distinguish their words.

They were speaking of certain vessels which would arrive most likely before sunrise; of yet more troops to come, and before having passed out of earshot referred to the defenceless position of our fleet at Presque Isle, although not putting it as strong as was the fact.

All this my father knew full well from rumors which had been brought to him by the people round about, and also through messages sent by General Porter of Black Rock.

We had gained nothing especial save the confirmation of his fears, and it surely seemed as if now was come the moment when we could discover all it was necessary our people should know.

Such thought was in my mind when Alec pressed my arm to attract attention, and motioned that we follow the group.

I was not averse to obeying him, for at that moment danger was forgotten.

It was not a simple matter to thus play the part of spies successfully, and in order to avoid discovery we were forced to remain at such a distance in the rear that only now and then was it possible to catch a word of the conversation.

Intent on discovering the time set for the attack, we became more heedless, and gave attention only to those in advance, when, without the slightest warning, we came full upon a squad of soldiers most likely sent out to relieve the sentinels.

So near were we to these redcoats before they discovered us, or we them, that I might, by stretching out my hand, have touched the foremost, and for an instant they must have believed us a portion of the force from the encampment.

One of them hailed us in a friendly manner, asking where we were bound, and another continued on as if to pass us by.

Had we been quicker witted I believe there was a chance of giving them the slip; but our silence, and the attempt on Leon's part to make his way into the bushes, betrayed us.

The man nearest touched me on the shoulder, and with the weight of his hand there came into my mind full knowledge of the imminent peril which threatened. Taken prisoners now, it was reasonable to suppose some one might recognize us as the lads who had been captured three months before, and there could no longer be any question but that we were spies.

It would be almost certain death to yield, and the position of affairs could not be rendered worse by resistance.

"We must never be taken!" I said half to myself, and for an instant it was as if I had in my arms the strength of a dozen men.

Wresting, by a sudden movement, the musket from the hands of the man who would have made me his prisoner, I struck out right and left, and in an instant we three lads were fighting desperately, as will even rats when they find themselves cornered.

CHAPTER VII.

IN HIDING.

IT is impossible for me to describe of my own knowledge all that took place during five minutes or more after I grappled with the Britisher.

There had been no thought in my mind, when I leaped upon the enemy, of gaining a victory; I was conscious only of the fact that if we were taken prisoners again our lives would pay the forfeit, because it must be apparent to all that we were spies, else why had we ventured there the second time; and I acted upon the impulse of the moment.

Had my companions been told in advance of what I proposed to do, they could not have followed my example more promptly.

It seemed as if almost at the very second that I seized the redcoat's musket, they made an attack, each upon the man nearest him, and so unexpected was the onslaught that the Britishers gave no outcry.

I remember that during what seemed to me like many moments I struck out, or parried blows, giving no heed to the weapon I had first seized, and that we fought desperately in silence until my opponent suddenly fell when I was some distance from him.

Then I realized dimly that he had been stricken down from behind, and an instant later Alec whispered hoarsely, as he grasped me by the hand: —

"Come, now! In ten seconds more it will be too late!"

I failed to understand all his meaning; but, fortunately, had sufficient sense to obey the strain upon my arm, and immediately we were in full flight, plunging through the underbrush without any idea, on my part at least, of where the course might lead.

Then as we ran I became conscious of the fact that Leon was leading the way, and for the first time since we stumbled upon the soldiers I had hopes that we might finally escape.

We ran at full speed, stumbling here over fallen trees, or floundering there through bogs and swamps, holding the pace until it became impossible for Alec to advance another yard.

"I am done up!" he panted, sinking down at the foot of a huge pine tree. "Do not stop; but leave me here to take my chances!"

"Can you go no further?" I asked stupidly, for

it was plain to be seen that the lad's strength was entirely spent.

"Not a step; but neither you nor Leon can afford to loiter. You two should be able to give them the slip."

"I have no idea of leaving a comrade," I said, flinging myself down by Alec's side to show the dear lad that I was not minded to desert him, and Leon followed my example, saying as he did so:—

"The English may as well have three prisoners as one, and I will remain with those who rescued me from the lake."

"But you are to do nothing of the kind!" I cried in alarm, thinking of the lad's mother, whose only support he was. "You can contrive to gain home secretly, knowing the country as you do, and in the morning no one will be able to say you were with us. Go, Leon! You must not sacrifice yourself!"

"That is what I should be doing if I deserted a friend. We will remain here, and it may be the soldiers will fail to find us."

It was possible they might pass us by in the darkness, unless we betrayed our whereabouts by thus wrangling as to who should go or stay, and I fell silent at once, understanding at the same time that words were of no avail in the effort to persuade the French lad into deserting us.

We three remained motionless as statues, and quite as silent, save for our heavy breathing, which could not at once be stilled, until, as the moments passed, we understood that the pursuit was either abandoned, or the soldiers had gone in the wrong direction.

We had escaped, for the time being at least, and my surprise was very nearly akin to fear as I realized this, for it seemed little short of miraculous that such good fortune could come to us.

"They must be hiding near by, ready to leap upon us the instant we leave this thicket," I said half to myself, and then I knew that Alec was laughing heartily, although silently.

"Do you suppose the Britishers would be willing to sit down and wait patiently until we were rested?" he asked, pressing my hand warmly. "We have given them the slip, Dicky Dobbins, and you shall have the full credit of it, because save for your bravery it might never have been brought about. I should have been clapped into that same pen where we nearly froze to death, before having the courage to engage half a dozen soldiers in a hand-to-hand fight!"

"Nor would I have shown so much bravery had there been time in which to think of the danger. The fit came upon me quite by accident, and even at this moment I cannot tell what took place."

"Well, I can," Alec replied, still laughing silently. "You leaped like a tiger upon one of the men, wresting his musket from him, and Leon and I could do no less than follow the example. The soldier was twice your size, and yet you floored him with a single blow — "

"One of you did that, striking the fellow from behind," I interrupted. "But for your assistance I should speedily have been worsted."

"It was your third opponent that Leon felled with a blow from the butt end of a musket. You had tumbled two over, and was engaged with the third when I had an opportunity of seeing what was being done. I always believed you a courageous lad, Dicky Dobbins, but never have I supposed it was in your power to handle your fists with such skill."

Now although it may appear like boasting to repeat what I did all unconsciously on that night, it seems necessary to set down what Alec and Leon claim were my acts while in a frenzy of fear.

There were six soldiers in the squad we had run upon so unwittingly, and two of those I bowled over much as a skilful pugilist would have done, tackling the third just as my companions came to the rescue.

Leon had seized the musket I wrested from the first redcoat, and with it felled one man unaided;

then he knocked over the fellow who was trying to best Alec, and afterward aided me as I have said.

Even then, as we sat in the forest listening in vain for sounds of pursuit, it seemed incredible that we had won the day so easily, and during a full half hour we gloated over the victory.

Then, when it seemed certain the Britishers had not succeeded in keeping upon our trail, we began to realize that the danger, instead of having passed, was hardly more than begun.

We were on that long, narrow neck of land known as the North Foreland, and, as Leon said, the enemy had a line of sentinels stretched across the narrowest portion, nearest the main shore, to prevent desertions and keep the curious at a proper distance.

In other words, we were penned up with no means of escape save by water, and the lad upon whom we depended as a guide had entirely lost his bearings in the darkness.

"It is only a question of time before we will be captured," I said gloomily, when coming fully to understand the situation, "and we cannot live in the thicket many days without food!"

To this dispiriting remark Alec made no reply, and I believed the lad was disheartened until he said cheerily, and in much the same tone he might have used when discussing some excursion for pleasure : —

"We are captured to a certainty if we make up our minds to such a fact; but I have the idea that by a show of half as much pluck as you displayed when we were confronted by the soldiers, we can leave this point of land in due season."

"Perhaps you already see your way clear to get out of the snarl," I said, with a fine tinge of sarcasm in my tones.

"Ay, that I do," he replied, giving no heed to my ill temper. "In case you two are minded to follow my instructions, it will go hard indeed if we fail of setting sail in our boat between now and sunset to-morrow."

He spoke so confidently that I pricked up my ears at once, a new hope coming into my heart, and Leon said quietly, much as if he was safe from all harm, and we the only ones who had anything to fear from the Britishers : —

"I stand ready to do whatever you shall say."

"Then set about finding your home, leaving us here — "

"I cannot play so cowardly a part," he interrupted. "Anything else, and you have only to command me."

"It was not a part of my plan that you should desert us, my bold Frenchman; but in order that we get off you must be free to act. Suppose you succeed in reaching your home before daylight, what will be more easy than to provide us with food in case we are forced to remain some time in hiding? Then, again, should our boat be seized, you could do something toward procuring another. My only hope of escaping depends upon your being at liberty to go and come."

Now it was that I, as well as Leon, began to understand what Alec had in mind, and both of us caught eagerly at the chance, slight though it was.

"I could find my way even in the night if we stood on either shore of the point," the French lad said, half to himself, and Oliver Perry's brother made answer, as if it was a simple thing to walk out of the thicket:—

"Tell me in which direction you wish to go, and I will lay out the course."

I should have made no reply to such a remark, believing my comrade was in jest; but Leon, whose faith in Alec seemed perfect, said quietly:—

"If we could gain the northern shore of the Foreland it would not be far to my home."

Alec stepped out from the thicket where he might gain a view of the sky, and after searching with his eyes as if hunting for some particular star, said in the tone of one who defies contradiction : —

"In that direction is the north; but, unfortunately, I cannot tell you how far we may be from the shore."

"It makes little difference; even though we were on the very southern edge I could gain my home before daylight. That which troubles me now is, where I am to find you again."

"We can easily settle the question. Dicky Dobbins and I will follow till we are come near to your mother's home, and then hide at some convenient place for a time."

"Why should you not enter my home?"

"For many good reasons, my friend. In the first place there is no question whatsoever but that the Britishers will make careful search for us as soon as sunrise, if not before, and most likely your home will be visited. In such a case there is little fear of your getting into serious trouble, because in the darkness I guarantee those soldiers did not see who made the attack upon them, and thus you will be free to wait upon us."

Now I began to understand more of what Alec would do, and straightway, after an unfortunate habit of mine, I at once believed it would be possible to better the plan.

"If we can make our way so far as Leon's home, what prevents us from going directly on board our boat? I have no desire to linger on the North Foreland, and surely there is nothing more to be learned regarding the movements of the enemy."

"Nothing would please me better than to set sail within the hour; but according to my thinking we had best keep away from the shore during this night at least, for if the Britishers have sentinels near to the mainland to prevent any one from coming upon the point, they know beyond a question we arrived in a boat of some kind, and most likely men are searching for our craft, if they have not already found her. After sunrise Leon can easily learn the condition of affairs, and thus we shall avoid running unnecessarily into danger."

I was not thoroughly convinced that this would be the wisest course, for it seemed to me better that we take some chances with the hope of getting away speedily, than to linger where there was so much of danger.

However, I said nothing, luckily, else would I have been put to shame two or three hours later, when we were come near to where Leon lived.

Alec gave the lad the proper course, as I have said, and held him to it so truly by observing the stars from time to time, that considerably before midnight we were standing where we could distinguish the outlines of the coast at a point, as the French lad declared, within three miles of his home, and so far from the encampment that there was little fear of coming upon the redcoats, unless, peradventure, squads of them were out in search of us.

From this point our advance was a reasonably rapid one, the guide striking a path through the thicket which he knew full well, and when we had come within five hundred yards, as he declared, of the dwelling, Alec said, coming to a halt:—

"We two will stop hereabout, and do you go ahead, Leon, to learn if the soldiers have visited the house."

All this seemed to me like an excess of precaution, for there was nothing to be heard save the ordinary noises of the night in the forest, and I could see no reason why we should not make ourselves as comfortable as possible, at least until daybreak.

Leon, having every faith in Alec's judgment, did not delay; but went on swiftly, leaving us alone, and there we remained until it seemed positive to me the French lad had abandoned us.

More than once I would have spoken with my comrade, urging some such possibility, but that he, pressing his hand over my mouth whenever I made the attempt, thus ensured silence, and the darkness of night was beginning to give way slightly to the coming day when Leon finally returned.

He had in his arms a bulky package, and when I sprang up to meet him intimated by gestures that I should remain quiet.

Then cautiously, and in the most careful whispers, he told what proved to me once more that I was in no wise fit to direct the movements of even myself while in an enemy's country.

The soldiers came to his home within half an hour after he arrived, while his mother was making ready the provisions for us which he had just brought.

They demanded to know why the household was astir at such an unseasonable hour, and she, without absolutely telling an untruth, gave them to understand it was because her son, who had been forcibly taken from her the night previous, had but just returned.

Then Leon was forced to submit to the most searching questioning as to how he had escaped from the bateau, and who had brought him to the North Foreland.

He told only the truth in replying to these questions, but did not tell it all.

Two young men, he said, had found him at the mercy of the wind and waves, and yielding to his earnest entreaties, set him ashore near the easternmost end of the point.

When the men asked concerning the two strangers, Leon professed to know nothing, believing it was right to speak an untruth rather than give up to their enemies those who had befriended him.

From what was said during the three hours this searching party remained in Leon's home, the lad and his mother understood that every effort would be made to prevent those who had assaulted the soldiers from leaving the point, and to that end sentinels were stationed along the shore.

It was believed by the Britishers that those who had brought Leon home were spies, and threats were freely indulged in as to what fate would overtake them once they were captured.

Whether our boat had as yet been discovered we had no means of knowing; but it did not seem probable that those who visited Mrs. Marchand's home had found the craft, otherwise some mention would have been made of the fact.

Now it was that I realized how wise Alec had been in preventing me from going directly to the farmhouse, and what would have been our fate had I carried out my purpose of attempting to embark without first making certain where the Britishers might be.

Taking it all in all our position was as disagreeable as it well could be.

From what Leon had heard we knew that the North Foreland would be rigorously searched next morning, and also that there was little opportunity of our being able to take to a boat, at least within the next four-and-twenty hours, while the chances were decidedly against our having a craft which we could call our own after the sun had risen.

The French lad, repeating again and again that he was ready to do whatsoever we might desire of him, said that his mother advised he should not linger with us many moments, lest the Britishers, suspecting him of knowing more than he admitted, might have sent some one on his trail.

Therefore it was that he seemed eager to be gone, and when he had led us to a sort of cave, and yet which was hardly more than an excavation under an overhanging rock, Alec said to him : —

"It is well that you leave us; and remember, Leon, we don't expect to see you again until the danger is well-nigh past. With such an amount of food as you have brought, and the possibility of getting water during the hours of darkness, there is little likelihood of our suffering while we remain in hiding. Therefore go back; stay around home as you would under ordinary circumstances, and keep your eye out now and then to see if the enemy discover our boat."

"I will return at midnight to-morrow," Leon said, moving slowly away; and I understood that had the lad consulted his own inclination he would not have left us.

"Do not come unless it seems certain the redcoats believe we two have given them the slip. No good can be effected by your visiting us more often than is absolutely necessary."

"But the time will drag heavily on your hands," he suggested; and Alec replied, with a laugh: —

"It will pass a deal more swiftly than if we were confined in such a prison as the Britishers have on this point of land, and that both Dicky and I know by painful experience. Go now; keep your ears open for any information which may be of importance to our purpose. After what you have suffered, the king's soldiers can be no friends of yours. Then, when your mother believes it is safe to venture out, come with what will be cheerful tidings."

Leon clasped each of us by the hand, and then, as if fearing to trust himself to further speech, walked rapidly away, and we were alone in hiding; with no friends on all the North Foreland save the French lad and his mother.

By this time we were needing both food and sleep, therefore we did not at first realize how tedious might be the confinement in our narrow hiding-place.

It was, as I have said, little more than an excavation under an overhanging rock; but the opening was so small that it had the appearance of being a veritable cave, and was partially screened from view of those who might pass, by a few small shrubs. The interior was hardly more than large enough to admit of our lying at full length, and in no place could we stand upright.

All these things were noted in a general way, and it was not until after many hours had passed that we realized to the full how cramped a prison it might prove.

The shore of the lake — that is to say, such portion of the Foreland as was washed by the narrow strip of water which lay between the point and the main — was not above three hundred yards distant, and Alec proposed that we hurry down and drink our fill while it was yet dark, for after the day dawned it would not be safe to venture forth.

This we did, and having returned, made a hearty meal from the provisions Leon brought.

Before the repast was come to a close the shadows of night had been dispelled by the rising sun, and we were prisoners until darkness should screen us once more.

I proposed that, having plenty of time at our disposal, we both indulge in slumber, but to this my comrade would not listen.

It was necessary, he believed, that one of us keep constant watch, lest the enemy should come while we were unconscious, and the sound of our heavy breathing might betray the secret of the hiding-place.

He insisted that it should be his duty to stand guard, as he termed it, during the early part of the day, and held to this point so stoutly that I could do no less than take my first turn at sleeping.

Now, although we knew full well how great was the danger, and realized that at any moment we might find ourselves in the hands of the enemy, who would surely put us to death as spies, fatigue bore so heavily upon me that my eyes were no more than closed before sleep came, and during a certain time I rested as sweetly and profoundly as if safe in my father's house at Presque Isle.

When I awakened the sun was riding high in the heavens, and Alec, sitting near the opening of the cave just behind the clump of bushes, was keeping careful watch.

" Do not reproach yourself for having slept while

there was an opportunity," he said, when I would have made excuses for taking my ease so long, leaving to him all the labor. "When the moment comes that we make a dash for liberty, it may be necessary to keep our eyes open many hours on a stretch, and by dividing the watches, if it so be we have the inclination, one or the other can sleep all the time."

It was good proof that the dear lad needed rest when, having once stretched out at full length, his eyes closed almost immediately in slumber, and during at least an hour I do not believe he so much as moved hand or foot.

At the end of that time I ceased to watch my sleeping comrade, for the tramp of footsteps and the hum of voices could be heard just outside the cave, and I knew beyond a peradventure that the Britishers were searching for us.

Unless they were doing their work most carelessly, it did not seem possible they could pass the aperture without discovering it, for of a verity, if I had been searching for a fugitive, I would have taken good care to know what might be under such an overhanging rock as marked the entrance to our place of refuge.

For an instant there came into my mind the thought that it was necessary Alec be awakened in case the

K

men came upon us, and I stretched forth my hand to touch him; but drew it back immediately when the sound of voices told that they had halted directly in front of where I sat, not more than ten paces away.

CHAPTER VIII.

A CLOSE SHAVE.

I NEEDED no evidence to convince me that the Britishers would make every effort to capture us. It was the one thing necessary for them to do, even though they could not hope to keep secret the fact of their encampment here on the North Foreland.

Whoever was in command of the troops must have known beyond a peradventure that the Americans living on the opposite shore of the lake had certain knowledge regarding the gathering of soldiers at this point, for the camp was already established on that winter's afternoon when Alec and I ran blindly into the hands of the redcoats.

From what we heard while held as prisoners so many weeks previous, my comrade and I knew that a movement was contemplated before the ice broke up.

Why it had been delayed we might never learn to a certainty, but it seemed positive to me at this moment —for when danger was so imminent the veriest trifles passed through my brain with lightning-like rapidity

—that instead of abandoning the manœuvre it had simply been delayed, in which case secrecy was even more necessary now than when we came so unwittingly upon the enemy.

In other words, that my meaning may be more plain, I understood at the moment that it was in the highest degree important to the enemy that we two lads be prevented from carrying any information back to Presque Isles, and, therefore, did I realize that the Britishers would spare no labor in the effort to take us prisoners.

The soldiers were advancing without heed as to noise, and before they were come so near that I could distinguish the words of their conversation, Alec awakened, looking toward me as if on the point of asking some question.

On the instant my hand covered his mouth, and the quick-witted lad needed nothing further by way of explanation.

With a motion of the hand he let me know that the situation was fully understood, and arose to a sitting posture as I removed the pressure from his mouth, the voices of our enemies speedily telling the whole story.

Nearer and nearer came the men, until we could distinguish every word that passed between them.

Instead of talking about the possibility of capturing

us, they spoke of the vessel which had arrived during
the night just past, and questioned why the other
craft were delayed when the wind was in their
favor.

We soon came to understand that the time for the
expedition to move was near at hand, and the blood
literally boiled in my veins as I believed that the attack would be made while we were thus virtually
prisoners.

Although apparently deeply engrossed by the topic
of conversation, the search was not being conducted
in any slipshod fashion.

From the sounds we knew that every bush sufficiently large to shelter us was being examined, and
it was not probable we could escape detection.

In less than five minutes the soldiers would have
come to the mouth of the cave, and our capture was
positive.

After that had been accomplished, a shameful death
would speedily follow for us, and the cold dew of fear
covered my forehead as I saw, in fancy, the last acts
in our lives. For an instant it was as if I already
stood upon the scaffold, and then Alec broke the horrible chain of thought which was making of me a wo-
ful coward.

He, dear lad, must have had the same mental pictures before him as were distressing me, for, leaning over until his cheek rested against mine, he clasped both my hands.

It was a mute farewell; the soldiers were so near that it seemed as if they must be upon us before one could count ten, and I shut my eyes, fearing to see what I believed was inevitable.

It seemed as if the men were standing within half a dozen paces of us, shut out from a view of the cave by the fringe of bushes which screened the entrance, when suddenly from the distance we heard a hail:

"This way! Quick! I have found traces of those whom you are seeking!"

It was Leon Marchand's voice, and both Alec and I knew the lad was imperilling his own life in the poor hope of being able to save ours.

I came near to crying out that he should think only of himself, leaving us to such fate as might be in store, so eager was I that he cease efforts which seemed to promise only danger for himself, without a chance that we might be benefited, and then was shown me how foolish is he who would try to change, by even so much as a hair's-breadth, the course of events.

The soldiers were not so foolish as to run at his summons; but halted where, by advancing a single pace, the search would have been ended, and began to parley with him.

"What have you found?" one asked, and the lad replied : —

"Only what appears to be a trail, but it leads toward the water."

I heard one of the men propose that they go back to investigate the matter; but a second called attention to the fact that they had been ordered to make certain no one was concealed within the line marked out, and with this difference of opinion came a parley which finally resulted in the saving of our lives.

The soldiers argued one with another, in the meanwhile moving nearer the point from which Leon was calling, and each second of time seemed to lessen our peril.

"Now has come the moment when we must make a move of some kind!" Alec said, clutching me by the arm fiercely to be certain I gave due weight to his words. "Leon can delay them only a few moments, and once they return to the search we are lost! It is better to make a venturesome move than be caught here like rats in a trap."

"But how can we benefit ourselves?" I asked stupidly. "It will be only an exchange of hiding-places, for there is no possibility of our leaving the shore in the daytime."

"That remains to be proven. It is almost certain death to stay here, and can be no worse to make a bold dash."

While speaking he literally pulled me to my feet, and as I stood near the entrance to the shallow cave only partially hidden by the bushes, I heard Leon cry : —

"Since you have declared that I am in league with those who saved my life when you would have taken it so cruelly, it is only fair to give me the opportunity of proving that I have spoken truly. Here is a trail, and if you neglect to follow it I shall insist that through your carelessness or wilfulness the spies escaped!"

It was this threat which stirred the soldiers to decided movement, and an instant later the sound of hurried footsteps told that they were moving in his direction.

The most flimsy of tricks had availed to save our lives, and it would be worse than folly if we failed to avail ourselves of the opportunity which might never occur again.

"Come!" Alec whispered, pulling me yet nearer the mouth of the cave. "At the worst we can only be captured, which is what must surely happen if we stay here."

"Where would you go?" I asked, giving rein to the cowardly fear which had beset me when death seemed so near.

"We can at least follow them up. Having searched for a certain distance, it is not likely they will go over the same ground twice, and the slightest cover will avail us, providing it be beyond this place."

Alec's manner of speaking, which was really little less than a command, acted upon me in proper fashion.

I recognized the fact that he was the true leader, and ceased to question, which was what I should have done in the first place.

"Come on," I said, now as eager to be in motion as I previously had been to hang back, and he lost no time.

In the distance we could hear Leon urging the soldiers to come to him, doing so solely for the purpose of giving us this poor opportunity to make the venture.

Alec ran swiftly, but with exceeding caution, directly back on the heels of the men, until we had gone perhaps fifty yards, and were so near that further advance would have been dangerous, when, striking sharply off to the left toward the shore, he increased the pace.

Thinking of the venture now, it seems well-nigh incredible that we should have succeeded in giving the Britishers the slip at the very time when they had us almost within their clutches; yet so it was permitted that we should do, although not without much difficulty and great danger.

Twice before gaining the shore we came near to running full upon one 'or the other of those who were being lured by the French boy's voice, and how we succeeded in escaping them it is impossible for me to say.

I only know that we did, and that after what seemed a very long time of scrambling over the fallen rocks, or wading waist-deep through bogs, we came out upon the northerly side of the Foreland.

Involuntarily halting just within a fringe of bushes which marked the limit of the water, I again asked myself helplessly of what avail was it that we had exchanged one hiding-place for another, since it seemed impossible, while being followed so closely, that we could embark.

Alec, brave lad that he was, did not hesitate because we had apparently come to the end of our path; but, pushing on in the direction of where we believed had been left our boat, he led the way at his best pace, and after five minutes or more had passed, the voices of our enemies sounded farther and farther in the distance, until even to my cowardly heart came the assurance that again we had earned a respite, although for how long no one could say.

Alec's will was stronger than his body, and while I was yet comparatively fresh it became necessary for him to make a brief halt in order to regain his breath.

"What now?" I asked, showing by the question that I recognized him as the rightful leader.

"I wish I might make answer in proper fashion," he said, with the ghost of a smile; "but it is a matter of chance. If it so be that Leon arouses the suspicion of our enemies, instead of leading them on a false scent, we are undone. But there yet remains the possibility that being convinced he has deceived them, whether wittingly or not, they will return without much search to the point at which he interrupted them, and in such case we may go free for the time being. My only hope now is of finding a craft of some kind."

It was on the end of my tongue to say that it would be foolish to make an attempt at crossing the lake in a common skiff; but I realized that anything was preferable to the certainty which awaited us if we remained on the Foreland, and held my peace.

We set out again, proceeding in the direction of Leon's home as nearly as might be; but meanwhile keeping within sight of the shore, and before another ten minutes had passed we saw, hauled up among the bushes as if with some attempt at concealment, a bateau in which were two paddles.

"That boat was left here by Leon," Alec said in a positive tone. "He brought her around from his home in the hope of gaining our hiding-place before the soldiers could arrive, and it only remains for us to push off, taking the chances that the weather holds good until we reach Presque Isle."

"That is little less than madness," I said decidedly, clutching him by the arm as if it was my purpose to prevent his carrying into execution any such plan as was intimated. "With half a gale of wind between here and the opposite shore we should be swamped to a certainty."

"And whether the wind blows high or low we are doomed if we stay here, for it is not likely we shall be so fortunate as to escape the searchers the second time."

I would have protested, even though conscious of the fact that we had best run any risk rather than remain, but he gave me no opportunity.

"We shall make the venture," he said, and laying

hold of my shoulders pushed me on in front of him as he ran speedily to the water's edge.

That we might set out from the shore and escape being seen by those on board the vessels lying near at hand, I did not believe, and left to myself I should have remained to take the poor chances on shore.

It was my comrade who saved me.

Literally forced to do his bidding, I pushed the bateau off from the land, leaping into her as she was water-borne, and in another moment we two lads were paddling for dear life, following the line of shore in that direction which would lead us around the point of the Foreland, from which place we might lay a straight course toward the American side of the lake.

Lest I make too many words of this harmless although disagreeable adventure, it is necessary I hasten over what at the time seemed to Alec and I like a most thrilling experience, although, as in other cases, we came to look upon it as something of but little moment.

We paddled along the shore of the Foreland within musket-shot distance, and neither heard nor saw anything of the enemy until we had rounded the point, when the British fleet lay fair before us.

Now was come the time when I believed we should be checked — when we would speedily find ourselves in the hands of those whose duty it would be to inflict upon us the punishment due to spies.

As we afterward learned, it was only the forwardness of their preparations which prevented them from giving heed to the bateau that was being urged farther and farther out into the lake, while apparently continuing on a direct course.

Between the British vessels and the shore, boats were constantly plying, carrying, as it seemed to us, full loads of soldiers; and we doubted not but that the long-deferred attack upon Presque Isle was about to be made.

"Knowing that two lads answering to our description came from the American shore, it is not likely we shall pass unchallenged," I said, and Alec replied with so much of cheerfulness in his tones that it heartened me wonderfully.

"There is much the same idea in my mind, Dicky Dobbins; but having succeeded in setting sail when it seemed positive we should fail to find an opportunity of leaving the shore, it is not seemly to look ahead in search of trouble. We can do no less than paddle at our best pace until some one does hail us, and then comes the question as to whether we can afford to disobey the command to put about. But for the fact that since we landed you have shown yourself to be a wondrously brave lad, I should say that you were in danger of growing cowardly."

"I have already become a coward; and as for showing myself brave, it is not true. Any fellow will fight for his life when he is cornered, and that is all I have done thus far. But for the fact that you forced me to put off in this boat, I should now either be in the hands of those who are searching for us, or skulking along the shore somewhere, with good show of being speedily discovered."

It is not to be supposed that we ceased our labor at the paddles while thus speaking.

On the contrary, even as I acknowledged my cowardice I redoubled my efforts, and the bateau sped over the water at a faster pace, I venture to say, than ever she had before.

Well, strange as it may seem, we passed the fleet almost within hailing distance, and yet apparently no attention was paid to us.

Within half an hour after rounding the point we were so far from the starting-point that even I had little fear we would be overhauled while the wind remained from the quarter it was then blowing, and a second time had we made good the flight from the North Foreland when the Britishers might, by exercising due caution, have prevented it.

Any other than Alec Perry would have taunted me with the fact that but for his efforts we probably would have met our death as spies.

He said not one word regarding his share in the escape; but contented himself with congratulating me upon what I had done against my own will, and as the moments wore on into hours we lost sight of the enemy's fleet.

It was a tedious journey which we made in the light bateau across the lake, having neither food nor water, and yet we would have been ungrateful lads indeed had any word of discontent passed our lips, for what was hunger, thirst, or fatigue as compared to that which would have been our lot had the Britishers captured us while we were within their lines?

More than once did we speculate upon how Leon Marchand might have settled matters with the soldiers after he had diverted them from the pursuit, and it was only when we thought of him that our hearts were heavy, for it was not impossible that by saving us he had jeopardized his own life.

Within twenty hours from the time of embarking in the bateau we were come to Presque Isle bay, and were there halted by the guard-boats which patrolled the entrance, for already had word been brought by those friendly to our people that the enemy were making ready to advance from the North Foreland.

If Alec and I had expected to be made much of on our arrival we were disappointed.

Those who acted as sentinels guarding the channel of the harbor gave but little heed to us, once having made certain we had a right to enter, and on landing it was as if all the people were panic-stricken.

Everywhere could we see the inhabitants moving their household goods toward the interior. Surely the town was being evacuated! Women, children, and even men, ran here and there frantically, and one would have said a sudden fear of death had come upon all.

We sought in vain for my father, believing he would be on shore, and the first man who was sufficiently calm to answer our questions told us that all who could be of service in manning the war-vessels were at their post of duty.

"What is come upon the people, sir?" Alec asked. "It would seem as if all had great cause for fear."

"So they have; and you must be a stranger here not to know that at noon yesterday the British set out from the North Foreland with a large force to destroy this town."

L

"We are but just come from there," Alec said quietly, "and know that at the time you mention the fleet was not ready to set sail."

Now the man regarded us more intently, and recognizing me as Captain Dobbins's son, asked sharply:

"Is it true that you are but just come from the Canadian shore?"

"Ay, sir. We were sent to spy upon the Britishers, and were near to falling into their hands. It may be they have begun by this time to cross the lake, but less than four-and-twenty hours ago we can answer for it that they remained inactive at the encampment. I had thought to find my father ashore, otherwise we would have sought him on one of the vessels."

"He went aboard the *Lawrence* less than two hours ago."

It was one of the brigs to which the gentleman referred; she had been named, by order of the Secretary of the Navy, in honor of the gallant captain of the *Chesapeake*, who gave his life for his country.

I would have gone home before endeavoring to find my father, in order that mother need not worry concerning us; but by this time several of the townspeople, overhearing what Alec said, had halted near by, and all of them demanded that we carry our information without delay to Captian Perry, urging that it was of vital importance he should know how matters stood on the North Foreland.

Therefore it was that within ten minutes after landing we embarked on the bateau again, and pulled for the opposite shore toward Little Bay, where the *Lawrence* was lying at anchor.

It is not necessary I should repeat what was said during the interview we had with Captain Perry and my father, neither of whom had given much heed to the rumors that an immediate attack was to be made upon Presque Isle.

Owing almost solely to the panic among the people, they had put our little fleet in such a state of preparation as was possible, but both understood that if the Britishers were near at hand some word must perforce be brought in advance.

Captain Perry questioned us closely concerning what we had seen on the North Foreland, appearing disappointed because we had failed to hear more of the conversation between the soldiers regarding the coming of the vessels which the Britishers expected; and then my father pinned us down to a most careful estimate of the time which had passed since we embarked on the bateau, after which Alec's brother said:—

"You lads are at liberty until you have made

ready to report on board here for duty. Our force is so small that every person, whether man or boy, must be ready to do a full share of such work as may fall to his lot."

Then we two were left to our own devices, and by talking with such members of the brig's crew as were acquaintances — for we had no idea of going on shore while we might remain aboard the *Lawrence* — we learned what had caused the commotion among the townspeople.

It was known even by the sailors that while the Government at Washington had failed to furnish Captain Perry with the force which was needed to man his fleet, orders had come for him to coöperate with General Harrison, although it was absolutely impossible to take even one of the brigs out of the harbor with so small a force.

We were told that reliable intelligence had been brought from Malden that the British had a new and powerful vessel there called the *Detroit*, which was ready for service against Presque Isle; also that Captain Robert H. Barclay, who had served with Nelson at Trafalgar, was in command of the fleet known to be cruising along the American shore.

Captain Perry, powerless to obey such commands as came from Washington, yet burning with the desire to strike a blow in behalf of his country, was forced to remain within the harbor on the defensive, when his one desire was to begin hostilities. With a force of sailors so small that the entire number would not have been sufficient to work the *Lawrence*, he could do no more than answer Commodore Chauncey's summons in the following words: —

"The enemy's fleet of six sail are reported off this harbor. What a golden opportunity if we had men! Their object is, no doubt, either to blockade or attack us, or to carry provisions or reënforcements to Malden. Should it be to attack us, we are ready to meet them. I am constantly looking to the seaward; every mail and every traveller from that quarter is looked to as the harbinger of the glad tidings of our men being on the way. Give me men, sir, and I will acquire both for you and myself honor and glory on this lake, or perish in the attempt. Conceive my feelings: the enemy within striking distance, my vessels ready, and not men enough to man them. Going out with those I now have is out of the question. You would not suffer it were you here. Think of my situation: the enemy in sight, the vessels under my command more than sufficient and ready to make sail, and yet obliged to bite my fingers with vexation for want of men."

CHAPTER IX.

A BLOODLESS VICTORY.

I HAD reckoned on setting down the details of
many small adventures which befell Alec and myself during such time as the townspeople of Presque
Isle were in a fever of fear, believing the British
would make a descent upon them while our fleet was
much the same as useless; but the pages are counting up so fast that many things must be omitted,
else I shall have come to an end of my paper before the real story has been begun.

Therefore it is that I may do no more than explain the condition of affairs in the settlement while
our vessels lay at their moorings inside the bar, useless, because lacking men, and the British frittered
away their time reconnoitring until, fortunately, we
were in fair condition to meet them.

After we two — meaning Alec and I — had brought
for the second time information of what was being
done on the North Foreland, and General Porter
sent word from Black Rock that the enemy's squadron

was about to make a descent upon us, there was neither man, woman, nor lad in the town who did not feel certain the attack must be made within a very few days at the longest, yet it was destined that we should have ample opportunity to make all necessary arrangements for defence.

Strange as it may seem, we were not molested for a space of three weeks, and to this day no person, save the British commander himself, has been able to decide why the king's forces did not destroy our little fleet, which afterward worked so much mischief.

As I have said, we expected momentarily to see the English squadron, and knew full well that it could not be successfully opposed by us; but yet we did not fold our hands in idleness.

The guard-boats at the entrance of the bay, just inside the bar, were redoubled, and orders given that three musket-shots should be fired when the enemy hove in sight.

The ship-carpenters were set at work building a blockhouse on the bluff east of Cascade Creek, to protect the shipyard, and such of the citizens as had not fled in terror were detailed to put up a redoubt on the heights commanding the bar, the same to be called Fort Wayne.

Captain Perry sent messengers to Major-General

Mead, at Meadville, asking that he order a body of militia to our aid with the least possible delay, and received from him the cheering intelligence that all men who could be spared should be set in motion at once.

The brigs and the schooners were moored near the shipyard, for no attempt at taking them over the bar was to be made until we had a sufficient number of sailors to man them; but the gunboats were fully armed, and anchored off Hospital Point, because, owing to their light draught, they could leave the bay at almost any time.

Alec and I, with many another lad, were ordered to labor at Fort Wayne; but it was understood that in case of an attack we should repair on board one of the gunboats without delay, and we knew that while the force of defenders was so small there would be no protest made, either by Captain Perry or my father, against our doing whatever might be possible in event of an engagement.

Such was the condition of affairs with us on the morning of July 21.

There was not an idler in the town, for the cowardly and indolent had long since fled to safer quarters, and as we worked with a will at whatever our hands found to do, every ear was pricked up for the signal which would tell that the enemy had at last decided to give us a taste of his quality.

Although expecting it, when the signal was sounded we were taken by surprise, so to speak.

It was nine o'clock in the morning when the reports of the muskets rang out on the warm, still air with a volume of noise which caused them to seem as loud as cannon, and the tools dropped from nearly every man's hands as he sprang to the highest point of land in order to gain a good view of the lake.

Alec Perry and I did not follow the throng that flocked to the summit of the heights; but, without so much as a single glance seaward, sped swiftly toward the old French fort, where we knew would be found a boat, and our only fear was lest the gunboats should leave the bay before we could board one of them.

We knew the enemy was in sight, otherwise the signal would not have been made, for Captain Perry had threatened direst punishment upon him who should give a false alarm, and we also believed the town would be speedily destroyed, for both my father and Alec's brother had privately said that we could not hope to successfully oppose the British squadron while our force was so small.

I do not set this down that it may be believed I felt unusually brave at the moment when it seemed certain Presque Isle was about to fall into the hands of the enemy, for at the time I gave no heed to possible danger.   My eagerness to be on board the gunboat overshadowed all else, causing me to forget for the moment what probably would happen, in the fear that it might be thought I remained on shore through cowardice.

"At last we shall have a chance to show that we can play the part of men!" Alec said, as we ran, and I, vain of the small share we had already taken in defence of our town, replied boastingly:—

"It seems to me that we have already done as much.   Who else can lay claim to having been twice inside the British lines?"

"Perhaps no one would care to admit being so foolish," he said, with a laugh.   "We might have been among the redcoats a dozen times, and yet it would count for but little if we had accomplished nothing more than has already been done."

"Was it not of some service when we reported the number of men on the North Foreland?"

"If such was the case neither your father nor my brother gave us any credit.   It strikes me they treated our adventures as childish pranks, rather than the work of men; but now the case will be different, for we are to help man the gunboat."

I might have reminded him that we probably would not remain long on board, once the enemy came within range, for the three small craft with which Captain Perry proposed to meet the British squadron were not calculated to make much of a fight against heavily armed, well-manned vessels of war; but I held my peace, for this was not the time to say what might possibly dampen his enthusiasm.

We gained the water's edge at the same moment as did my father, who had come from the barracks, and leaped into the boat close at his heels, I rejoicing that chance had thrown us in his company, since now we must serve under him rather than one of the other commanders.

"How many of the Britishers are in sight?" he asked of the man in charge of the boat, and the latter replied, as his crew pushed the light craft off from the shore: —

"I have not seen the fleet, sir; but it was said by those on Hospital Point, who had a full view of the lake, that there were six sail bearing directly down upon us."

"Is Captain Perry on board the *Tigress?*"

(This was the name of the gunboat on which it had been decided Captain Perry, as commodore of the fleet, should remain, and she was to be commanded by my father.)

"Ay, sir; but so weak from the fever as to be fitted for the hospital rather than to go into an action where we're like to be sunk offhand."

"He was feeling better last night."

"Yes, sir; but Dr. Parsons came ashore two hours ago to get some supplies, and I heard him say the captain was under the weather again."

"The prospect of going into action will brighten him up a bit, and I venture to say you will never hear him speak so discouragingly of the future as you have just spoken, not even though we were outnumbered twenty to one."

"That is about the odds we shall have against us, sir," the boatman said firmly, but decidedly, "and I allow it is not discouraging to others when a man looks at the situation as it really is, providing he does not show the white feather."

"I had rather hear you say that we're like to do the enemy serious harm, than to croak about his sinking us offhand."

"And how long, sir, with all due respect in the question, do you think we've a chance of standing against the British squadron?"

"Till we've given him a fair taste of our metal, that

I'll be bound!" my father replied emphatically; and then he turned to look seaward as if intimating that such profitless conversation had best come to an end.

Now it was that we caught a glimpse of the enemy, and that which we saw was by no means heartening.

Our boat, headed for the *Tigress*, had passed the range of Hospital Point, giving us an opportunity of looking out over the lake to the westward, and we saw the spars of no less than five vessels, two of them being ship-rigged.

To go out against them with three small gunboats each carrying a single gun, seemed much like the veriest folly, and I ceased to feel surprised at the boatman's belief that we would be sunk offhand.

Alec glanced at me meaningly when we had gazed at the enemy as long as was pleasant, and I read in his eyes nothing but delight that at last we were to do something more than act as spies or carpenters.

As for myself, I would have been well content to remain in safety on shore, although as a matter of course I should not have left my comrades had the opportunity offered; but I assumed a bold bearing, determined that my father might never so much as guess how timorous his son could be at times.

Nothing more was said by the occupants of our craft while we pulled to the gunboat, and I fancy that much the same thought must have been in the mind of every person, however bravely he may have spoken, for one would have been lacking in common sense to believe our three small vessels might give successful battle to such a squadron as now lay fair before us.

Once on board the *Tigress* we found so much to do that there was no opportunity for gloomy thoughts.

Although matters were supposed to be in proper trim, now that the decisive moment had arrived there were many details to be arranged, and Alec and I were kept running hither and thither, with this thing or that, while the gunboats were being gotten under way.

Although the fever had a firm hold upon him, Captain Perry was on deck superintending the work when we arrived, and despite all my father could say he persisted in remaining there, replying to every argument used against his presence : —

"If we could employ our entire fleet this day the malady would have wholly disappeared, and even as it is, when we are to put out in the face of such great odds, I am better both in body and mind than I have been since we left Buffalo."

The *Tigress* was fitted for one gun, and the piece was in position, under charge of Silas Boyd, an old man who was said to be the most skilful gunner among us.   In addition to this were two short carronades, temporarily placed amidships where they might be effective in repelling boarders, but could not be relied upon for anything else.

To the great pleasure of Alec and myself, we were detailed to assist old Silas, who would be chief gunner when the *Lawrence* was put in commission; and while we were advancing boldly toward the enemy, as if confident of achieving a victory, he gave us his final orders:—

"Them as belong to a gun's crew shouldn't stand around waitin' for the word to be given, but ought to know what is needed an' do it before a command can be given. Now you lads are to keep back after this 'ere gun is loaded; but the minute it's fired, you're to set about spongin', so the others won't be delayed in their part of the work."

"We are more than willing to do our share of the labor," Alec said, with a hearty laugh; "but it isn't to be supposed that we, who have never taken part in an engagement, will be able to anticipate your wishes."

"You'll come to it in time, lad, you'll come to it," old Silas said, as he stepped back a few paces and gazed at my comrade admiringly. "A boy who can laugh like that while the odds are so heavily against us will soon understand what's to be done when the action begins."

"It's as well to laugh as cry; and even though some of the men croak about the chances in favor of the enemy, I'm heartily glad the redcoats have decided to give us the opportunity of striking a blow, for it's dull work building forts on shore."

Old Silas gravely took Alec by the hand; and I would have given much had that mark of approbation been bestowed upon me by such a man as the gunner, for it meant more than words could have expressed.

Captain Perry ordered that the drums beat to quarters, although every man was in the position assigned him. There was to be no lack of formality simply because ours seemed like a forlorn hope.

The men cheered loudly when the roll of the drums ceased, and from the other gunboats we could hear the same token of satisfaction that we were at last bearing down upon the Britishers who had threatened us so long.

"There is no need to ask that every man will do his duty," my father said, as he advanced so far forward that all might see him. "We shall meet the enemy in whatever force he may come, and I do not fear any on board the *Tigress* will show the white feather!"

Another cheer went up; and then had come the

moment when my heart seemed to leap into my mouth, for the British fleet was standing down toward us, all the crews at quarters, and the guns showing grim and ominous from the open ports.

The ship *Queen Charlotte* was leading, and no attempt was made to form a line of battle. Most likely the redcoats believed we could be whipped so readily that there was little need of manœuvring for position.

"Fire when you think any execution can be done, Mr. Boyd," my father said, after Captain Perry had given the word; and the old man muttered, in a tone so low that only Alec and I heard the words:—

"I reckon I'm as near ready now as I ever shall be. This ere gun ought 'er carry that far, an' he who strikes the first blow has the best chance of gainin' an advantage."

One of the crew was standing near with a lighted match, and old Silas, after sighting the piece carefully, motioned that fire be applied to the priming.

There was a report as of thunder; the *Tigress* quivered from stem to stern; and out of the cloud of white smoke I saw the ball speed toward the foremost ship.

If Silas Boyd had never aimed a cannon before, his reputation as a skilful gunner was made from that

M

moment, for we saw the missile strike the *Queen Charlotte's* mizzenmast, sending from it a shower of white splinters, and causing the spar to sway to and fro as if on the verge of falling.

What a shout went up from our little fleet at this token of gunnery!

It was as if every man tried to outdo his comrade at making a noise; and in the midst of the tumult the other gunboats paid their respects to the Britishers by sending iron balls toward them, but none save that fired by old Silas struck its target.

So engrossed were Alec and I in watching the movements of those on board the wounded ship that we entirely forgot the part we were supposed to play, and stood idly by with the sponges in our hands until the old man cried angrily: —

"Get to work, you idlers! Did you come aboard only to gape around when there was work to be done?"

It can well be fancied that we leaped forward to do our duty, and at the instant of so doing I saw half a dozen wool-like puffs of smoke from the ship's side, which told that she was not intending to take our fire without making some return.

Once more our gun was loaded, and again old Silas squinted along the piece.

The match was applied to this second charge, and we saw the ball describe a half-circle against the sky; but the result was not the same.

The breeze had been freshening, and the *Tigress* rose on a wave at the instant the gun was discharged. This movement probably destroyed the aim, or the piece may not have been sighted as carefully; at all events, the missile fell ahead of the ship, and old Silas indulged in many an angry word because of his failure.

Alec and I did not give him an opportunity to remind us of duty again.

Instantly the ball struck the water we were at work with the sponges, and by the time the old man had finished shaking his fist at the enemy in impotent rage, the crew were engaged in reloading.

We had good cause for rejoicing, however, even though none of our people succeeded in sending a shot aboard the Britishers.

The increase in the weight of the wind brought down the wounded mizzenmast, and as it fell we saw go up on the *Queen Charlotte* signals which we soon learned was an order for the squadron to haul off.

Incredible though it may seem, the king's fleet turned tail when there were but three small craft, carrying only as many guns, to oppose them, and in less than ten minutes from the time Silas Boyd opened the one-sided battle, every vessel flying the British flag was scudding toward the Canadian shore!

We had actually beaten off the squadron, any single craft of which should have been more than a match for our three little gunboats, and that without having received a scratch!

It was several moments before we could believe that this really was the case, and then what a volley of cheers went up!

We could even hear the people on shore as they yelled themselves hoarse over this bloodless victory, and I was so foolish as to fancy that Captain Perry would give chase at once, for the sense of triumph was so great I believed our poor schooners a match for the redcoats.

"Can it be that we are going back?" I asked, in dismay, when the *Tigress's* head was turned toward the shore. "We have only to give them a few more shots in order to sink the whole fleet!"

"The smell of burnin' powder is gettin' into your head, lad," old Silas said, in a tone of reproof. "Don't run away with the idee that the Britishers won't, or can't, fight. We shall have proof of that later, and he would be a fool who should try to gain any more of an advantage than we've already got by sheer luck."

"They don't show any inclination to fight, whatever it may be possible for them to do!" I replied hotly.

"There's some good reason for it, you may be certain, although it ain't likely we'll ever know what it is. Let well enough alone, you young fire-eaters," he added, addressing Alec also, who by this time was giving audible vent to his displeasure. "It's satisfaction in plenty that we've driven 'em away, when it seemed sure we'd all be sent to the bottom, for I wouldn't have given a brass sixpence for our chances half an hour ago."

Having said this the old man turned toward his gun, as if he could not afford to waste more time on such as us, and we two lads watched in silent sorrow the enemy's vessels as they increased the distance between themselves and the American shore.

Before landing again, however, we came to understand that it would have been the height of folly for us to have pursued the squadron; but from that hour we, as well as the majority of our people, had more confidence in Captain Perry's ability to hold Presque Isle against the enemy.

"If the government would only send a force sufficient to man our vessels, we'd soon give the Britishers such a lesson as could not fail of proving that we hold control of this lake!" Alec said to me after a time. "Every vessel in the squadron would have been ours had we gone against them with the brigs!"

It was useless to keep repeating such ideas, and I held my peace. During the past two weeks they had been put into words by every man in Presque Isle, and yet no reënforcements arrived.

The vessels built to defend the coast were lying idle at their moorings, armed and provisioned; but useless because we could not raise sufficient force to so much as man one of them.

Alec and I went back to the work of fort-building; but now we had more stomach for the labor, because we had seen what might be done, and because we had greater faith in the qualities of our small force than was really warranted by the facts.

Two days after this encounter a sailing-master in the navy, by name of Champlin, arrived with seventy men, and our hopes arose once more, for now one of the brigs could be sent out if need arose, and we believed more sailors would speedily follow.

Captain Perry and my father, however, knew how vain were these hopes, for Master Champlin had reported to them that no more men were ordered to Presque Isle, and again Alec's brother pleaded for an opportunity to show what might be done with the fleet that had been built by frontiersmen.

As I came afterward to know, he wrote a second letter to Commodore Chauncey, in which he said: —

"For your sake and mine, send me men and officers, and I will have all the British squadron in a day or two. Commodore Barclay keeps just out of reach of our gunboats. The vessels are all ready to meet the enemy the moment they are officered and manned. Our sails are bent, provisions on board, and, in fact, everything is ready. Barclay has been bearding me for several days; I long to be at him. However anxious I am to reap the reward of the labor and anxiety I have had on this station, I shall rejoice, whoever commands, to see this force on the lake, and surely I had rather be commanded by my friend than any other. Come, then, and the business is decided in a few hours!"

CHAPTER X.

THE TRAITOR.

THE days passed, and nothing came of Captain Perry's second appeal for the forces which were needed if the United States would hold possession of the territory bordering on Lake Erie.

Alec and I, together with many other lads, worked industriously upon the fortification which had been named Fort Wayne even before anything was done toward building it, and I venture to say that if all the people in the United States had labored as earnestly on the defensive and offensive as did we of Presque Isle, the war would have been brought to an end before the close of the year 1813.

When we had put up the blockhouse on the bluff east of Cascade Creek, and finished the fort after a rude fashion, Major-General David Mead arrived at the head of a full regiment of militia, and then it seemed as if the government had at last remembered our feeble condition.

It was a day full of excitement when these troops entered the town, and not the least among the ceremonies was the saluting of the general with thirty-two guns as he went on board the *Lawrence* to pay his respects to Captain Perry, who, immediately after our late victory, had been brought low by a return of the fever.

My father was present at the interview; but what passed between the commanders we of the rank and file had no means of knowing, save as certain events transpired which we came to believe were the result of their deliberations.

It was only reasonable that, after having served under him, Alec and I should find it in our way to cultivate the acquaintance of Silas Boyd, and through him we got an insight into what otherwise would have been difficult for us to understand.

As for instance: The third day after General Mead's arrival men were set at work in the ship-yard on four huge scows, or box-like boats with flush decks, and my comrade and I puzzled our brains in vain to come at some reasonable conclusion regarding their purpose. It was evident they could never be intended for sailing crafts and equally certain that they were not being built for cargo-carrying, because there were no spars, and the upper portion was made without a hatchway, unless small square holes cut fore and aft might be called by such a name.

"They are boxes, rather than vessels," Alec said, after we had speculated long and vainly regarding their purpose, and then he added, as if the thought had but just come to him, "Let us learn if old Silas knows anything about them."

The gunner was not far off. He had just come ashore from the *Lawrence*, where he had been looking after some of the pieces which were not mounted according to his notions, and we summoned him without delay.

"Don't know the meanin' of 'em, eh?" he asked, with a laugh, after a brief survey of the odd-looking craft. "Well, lads, I'm allowin' that you'll be pleased because they've been begun."

"I can't understand why anything of that sort would give us pleasure," I said stupidly; but Alec, quicker witted, cried excitedly: —

"Do you mean that they have anything to do with our fleet leaving the bay?"

"Ay, lad, that's just the size of it, or I'm way off my reckonin'. I've seen such things before. They're called 'camels,' an' I've heard say it was the Dutch who invented them in order to carry vessels over shallow places."

Even now I failed to understand their purpose, and, seeing the questions in my eyes, the old man continued:

"Either of our brigs draws too much water to be taken out over the bar while the lake is as low as it is now — that much you'll allow. Later on, when these ere craft are built, an' Captain Perry is ready to put to sea, the brigs will be taken out as far as they'll float, an' these camels made fast alongside, fore an' aft. The water will be let into 'em through the port-holes in the sides an' deck, till they're sunk, after which beams will be passed from one to the other under the ship's keel. Then the hatches are put on again, an' battened down till the hulks are water-tight, after which the pumps are set to work. Now you lads know full well that once air takes the place of water, these scows will have considerable liftin' power, an' up goes the brig as a matter of course."

The old man paused as if thinking he had told all that was necessary; but I was so thick-headed that he was forced to explain every detail of the proposed crossing, although Alec probably did not need so much information because of understanding it thoroughly from the first description.

Until now I had failed to realize that the brigs could not leave the bay unaided until the water was higher, else I might have had even more fear regarding what it would be possible for the British to do; but after

such fact had been made apparent I saw great cause
for alarm.

"Suppose the enemy's squadron should come at the
very moment one of our vessels was trussed up on
those box-like camels?" I asked; and old Silas
shrugged his shoulders as he replied: —

"There is the chief danger, my lad; an' I'll answer
for it that your father an' Captain Perry have discussed
such a disaster again an' again since the lack of men
forced them to linger here until the water fell low.   If
the Britishers should come, there would be the end of
whatever craft might be on the bar at the time."

"Do you suppose others beside us know of what is
to be done?" I asked, anxiously.

"It stands to reason all do, lad, unless they are blind.
When such craft as these are bein' built, curious ones
are likely to ask the reason why."

As he spoke, there came upon me like a flash of
light what we had heard on the North Foreland that
winter's afternoon when Alec and I were held prisoners
in the narrow pen which was like to have been our
grave.   Then we learned, because of the information in
possession of the enemy, that among the people of
Presque Isle was at least one who stood ready to betray
us — one who was willing to sacrifice his neighbors in
order to curry favor with the Britishers.

I made mention of the fact to old Silas, telling him the whole story, and suggesting that the same person who had played the spy might yet be among us, but he laughed at my fears.

" Do you think the Britishers themselves could not play the spy ? I'll answer for it that more than one of their soldiers have been in this town since the keels of the vessels were laid, an' it is by such means that they were kept posted of our doings, not through treachery. I'll answer for it we haven't so mean a man among us."

The old man spoke so positively, and laughed so long at my fears, that I could not do otherwise than call myself a fool for having such suspicions, and straightway made every effort to put the matter from my mind.

Silas Boyd told us of many large ships which he had seen floated over bars by use of " camels," and otherwise gave so much interesting information concerning like engineering methods, that Alec and I listened to him eagerly until the day was spent, when we hastened to my home with all speed, lest mother should chide us for loitering when it was more seemly lads like us were snugly housed.

But even while most deeply entertained by the old gunner's stories, and when listening to my mother's loving words, the idea was ever present in my mind that among us was a traitor, who would speedily carry to the British information of the "camels" which were being made ready to take our vessels over the bar.

I said very little regarding this to Alec, lest he should make sport of me for being foolishly suspicious.

Perhaps because of my silence on the subject the thought grew stronger until it became the same as a fact in my mind, and I cast about trying to decide who among us was so lost to all honesty as to betray his own countrymen to their ruin.

When my father came home on this evening he reported that Captain Perry was more comfortable, as regarded the fever, and had given orders that Alec remain ashore until such time as commands were received for the fleet to leave port.

"And that is to be within a few days, if one may judge from the indications," the lad said, with a smile, when my father had reported his brother's words.

"Why do you think so?"

"Because of the camels which are being built at the shipyard."

"How knew you for what purpose those hulks were intended?" my father asked sharply, and, as I thought, with no little disquietude of mind.

As a matter of course it was necessary we should tell him all that had occurred during the day, and, having come to an end of our story, he said, half to himself : —

"I had hoped the people might not be quite so well informed."

"Why, sir?" I made bold to ask. "Think you any in this town would carry information to the enemy?"

"That I am not prepared to say, but with some people gold is a weighty argument, and has been known to buy the conscience of many an apparently honest man."

Then it was that I spoke of the suspicion which had been troubling me, and having come to an end, my father said reflectively : —

"Many have left Presque Isle since last winter, and it may be that among them was the one who then supplied the enemy with information. I do not recall to mind any who would play the spy, but yet there are several here whom I do not know sufficiently well to answer for their honesty."

"Is there no way by which such a possibility could be guarded against?" Alec asked, and my father replied : —

"We have taken due precautions. The guard-boats at the entrance of the bay will stop any craft attempting to put out into the lake without written authority signed by those in command, while the sentinels from here to Fort Wayne have orders to stop citizens trying to leave without a pass. Yet all these might be avoided by him who had it in his heart to work us mischief."

Such words as these were not calculated to set my fears at rest, and when Alec and I went to bed we discussed the matter in all its bearings, for since my father had spoken in such a tone I was not ashamed to give words to my fears.

However, we could do nothing more than talk, and in due course of time slumber put an end to all forebodings.

When morning dawned bright and clear I quite forgot the troubles of the previous night, and went with Alec to visit his brother on board the *Lawrence*.

Captain Perry was yet so ill that Dr. Parsons had forbidden his going on deck; but many officers were in his cabin when we arrived, and one could guess from the expression of gravity on the faces of all that some important subject was under discussion.

The captain greeted us in friendly fashion, inquiring solicitously after Alec's health; but after the first words of greeting had been spoken it might readily be seen that he was not anxious we should linger, therefore we took our leave after having been on board less than ten minutes.

Going on deck, we found old Silas bustling around as if charged with the most weighty missions, and I asked him laughingly if there was any chance the *Lawrence* would go over the bar that day.

Instead of replying in sportive fashion to my bantering, he suddenly became grave as any owl, and hurried away as if afraid he might be tempted to reveal a secret in case he remained with us.

"You may depend upon it that some movement is near at hand, and we are not to be trusted with even so much as an intimation of it," Alec said laughingly, as we went over the rail into our boat, which had been made fast alongside. "I am not disposed to grumble at being kept in ignorance, so long as we are soon to go out against the enemy, but I would enjoy knowing whether we are likely to miss anything by loitering on shore."

"It isn't probable the *Lawrence* will put to sea without us, after all the promises that have been made," I said, almost indignant with Alec because he should seem to question my father's good faith. "I am certain some hint would be given to us if anything of the kind were contemplated. Besides, it isn't possible the brig could be gotten over the bar in one day."

This last argument had more weight with my com-

N

rade than any other I could have advanced, and at once he lost all care as to what might be going on, bantering me to take a stroll with him along the shore to the eastward, where could be had a good view of the lake without a very lengthy journey.

"Who knows but that we may sight the bold Britishers before those in the guard-boats can do so, and thus gain considerable credit for being sharp-sighted!" he said sportively, and I took the words in good faith.

"We'll try it!" I replied so earnestly that he was provoked to mirth, and the boat's head was turned in the direction of Fort Wayne, in front of which fortification we landed when challenged by the watchful sentinel.

Once we were recognized there was no hesitation about allowing us to proceed whithersoever we pleased, and, as Alec had proposed, we directed our course along the shore of the lake.

Now it must be set down here that there was no thought in my mind that we could do more than possibly sight the enemy's fleet in the distance.

I had ceased to think there was a traitor among us, and, therefore, that which occurred came as much in the nature of a surprise as if there had never been any conversation between my comrade and myself regarding the chance that information concerning our movements might be carried to the Britishers.

We strolled aimlessly along the shore, talking of the time when our fleet should be out on the lake fully manned, and giving no heed to anything save what might be seen seaward, until Alec stopped suddenly, clutching me by the arm as he whispered: —

"Look just beyond that clump of bushes! Unless I am much mistaken there is a boat drawn up to prevent her from being seen!"

Many seconds passed before I could make out clearly that which had attracted his attention, and then I not only saw the craft, but distinguished amid the foliage the form of a man, who was peering through the branches at us.

"It is either a British spy, or the traitor who carried news to the enemy last winter!" I said excitedly, turning this way and that in the hope of seeing some one upon whom we could call for assistance.

Even as I spoke the fellow in hiding drew back until it was impossible to see so much as the outlines of his form; but Alec, rendered suspicious by a glimpse of the half-hidden boat, was ready to believe that I had made no mistake.

"It isn't likely a Britisher would venture here at this time, for there has been nothing of importance to attract one. It is some person from Presque Isle, who awaits an opportunity to set out across the lake, or has just returned," he said, now quite as excited as was I. "It is our duty, Dicky Dobbins, to make of that fellow a prisoner, in order that he may give reasonable excuse for behaving in such a fashion."

"There is little chance of our doing that without weapons, for be he spy or traitor, we can count on his making a good fight."

"No better than is within our power, if we are so disposed," Alec replied stoutly. "I have no idea of losing such an opportunity as is before us!"

Now I was quite as eager as he to learn who this man might be that he should thus take so many precautions against being seen ; but yet I believed we had good reason to be cautious in our movements lest we come to grief.

It was well that Alec Perry carried a stouter heart than mine, otherwise much of disaster might have come upon our little fleet before there had been an opportunity for Oliver Perry to show of what he was capable.

"Will you follow me ?" the dear lad whispered, and I replied, although decidedly against my better judgment : —

"Ay, that I will, Alec, although I believe you are running into danger needlessly. Why not wait until we can call others to help us, or at least get weapons with which to defend our lives, for if that fellow is either spy or traitor he will not yield without a fight."

"It is two against one, and even cowards could ask for no better odds than that!" Alec said sharply, and in another instant he was running at full speed toward the clump of bushes in which was hidden the man we would make prisoner.

There was no other course left me but to follow him, unless I was willing to have it said I deserted a friend, and even while reproaching myself for making such a foolhardy venture, I ran at my best pace close at his heels.

As a matter of course the stranger saw us coming, and whether guilty or innocent must have divined our purpose.

Perhaps the speed at which we advanced convinced him he could not outstrip us in a chase, for instead of taking flight, he made every effort to launch his boat before we should come up with him.

Had he succeeded in getting half a dozen yards from the shore we would have been baffled, weaponless as we were, and the fellow probably counted on this, but he had drawn the craft too high up on the sand.

She was less than ten feet from the water's edge when Alec came within striking distance, and now, instead of trying further to launch the boat, he turned to defend himself.

With a stout oaken paddle uplifted he awaited my comrade's approach, and I cried aloud in surprise when I recognized in him one of our neighbors who claimed to be violently loyal to the Government of the United States.

"It's Nathaniel Hubbard!" burst involuntarily from my lips, and as I spoke his name he turned upon me in a fury.

Until that instant I do not think there was in his mind any thought to do other than beat us off until he could set the boat afloat; but, finding himself recognized, it seemed necessary for his own safety that our mouths should be closed forever.

Stooping suddenly, he seized something from the bottom of the craft, and when he stood erect once more I saw in each of his hands a pistol.

"Look out for yourself!" I cried, fearing lest Alec had not observed the weapons, and even as I shouted there was a blinding flash; I could feel the heat of the burning powder, and wondered that no pain followed it.

Hubbard had fired point blank at me, within less than ten feet distance, and yet missed the target.

With a cry of rage he turned upon Alec, but before he could press the trigger of his pistol I leaped upon his back.

The weapon was discharged; but the bullet buried itself in the sand, and the traitor was at our mercy, although not yet conquered.

He fought like a wild man, and I could not wonder at his fury, for more than his life was at stake. Even though his neighbors did not kill him outright, as indeed they had good cause, he was disgraced forever; and there would be nothing left for him save to take refuge among those to whom he had sold himself, which might not be a pleasant thing, because he who buys a traitor can have no great respect or love for him.

During five minutes or more it was a serious question as to who would come off victorious, and then suddenly his strength seemed to desert him; he collapsed, so to speak, even while putting forth his greatest strength, and from that instant it was as if we had no more than a child in our grasp.

"We'll tie his hands and feet, and bundle him into his own boat," Alec said, whipping out his pocket-knife and cutting the small hempen cable, or painter. "It will be too much of a job to carry the scoundrel from here to the village!"

It was pitiful to see how weak the traitor had become in mind as well as body. Instead of making any protest, or challenging us to prove that he did not have as good a right as we to stroll on the shore of the lake, he burst into tears, imploring us to "be merciful."

"It can do you no good to take me back, and I will reward you richly for my liberty," he whined, in so cowardly a fashion that I turned my back, unwilling to look upon the despicable wretch.

"You will pay us with British gold, eh?" Alec said angrily, raising his hand, whereupon I seized his arm, fearing lest in his righteous wrath he might strike one who was bound, for we had lost no time in tying the fellow.

"Don't fear that I shall do him any great harm," the lad said quickly. "For a moment the temptation to punish him for thinking we might be bought was great, but I should have remembered in time that it would be a disgrace even to strike a cur who has sold his country."

From that instant Nathaniel Hubbard seemed to understand that it would be useless to plead with us.

He apparently gathered courage from despair, or else grief and remorse overpowered him, for he remained silent and motionless, seeming to give no heed whatsoever to us.

As if he had been no more than a bundle of merchandise, and not very valuable at that, we packed him into the boat and rowed back toward the brig whereon we knew was Captain Perry, feeling quite certain we had done a good forenoon's work in our country's behalf.

CHAPTER XI.

IF we lads had expected to be greeted with enthusiastic praises when we pulled alongside the *Caledonia*, near that portion of the deck where my father was standing, we were doomed to disappointment.

"Who have you there?" he asked sharply, not for the moment recognizing his old neighbor and professed friend.

"A spy whom we found on the lake front, having just come over, or about to put across," Alec replied, and I would have added more but that my father asked sternly : —

"How do you know he is a spy?"

"First, because of his suspicious movements when we hove in sight," Alec replied, still continuing to act as spokesman. "Dicky Dobbins and I went along the shore for a stroll, and, having come near to a clump of bushes grown close by the water's edge, saw a boat half concealed therein; also this man in hiding. When we came up he greeted us with two pistol bullets, and but for my comrade I would have been killed. Then, when we had him bound fast, he tried to bribe us into giving him his liberty. If all this be no token of his guilt, then am I much mistaken."

"It is Nathaniel Hubbard," I interrupted, understanding that as yet my father had not recognized the man.

"Nathaniel Hubbard!" he repeated. "And you have taken him for a spy?"

"If he was an honest citizen, sir, there would have been no such scene as I described," Alec said stoutly.

Perhaps if Master Hubbard had made any loud claim of innocence at this moment he might have been believed, so great was my father's confidence in the man. But, as I have already said, it was as if he collapsed entirely when we had gotten the best of him, and now could not utter a lie in his own defence.

Instead of giving us orders concerning the prisoner, my father wheeled abruptly around, disappearing almost immediately down the companionway, and I knew he had gone to acquaint Captain Perry with the painful intelligence that one of Presque Isle's most trusted citizens had proven himself a traitor.

We waited in the boat, Alec and I, until perhaps

ten minutes had passed, and then one of the guards
came to the rail and said : —

"The captain commands that the prisoner be taken
on shore by a force of men from the brig, and you
boys are to remain here."

Now it was that Nathaniel Hubbard found his
tongue. He who should have welcomed death as a
means of hiding him from view of those who had
trusted him, begged piteously for life, knowing full
well the people of Presque Isle would take the law
in their own hands once his perfidy was known.

"Pray to Captain Dobbins that I be confined on
board this ship!" he cried to the soldier who had
brought us the command. "Entreat him by the
friendship of former days not to deliver me into the
keeping of those who would shed my blood!"

Tears stood in the traitor's eyes, so great was his
fear, and I turned my head away, not caring to look
at that which was so disagreeable, for there was no
pity in my heart toward one who would sell his countrymen.

"Go, and repeat what he has said to Captain Dobbins," Alec commanded the soldier, and the latter
obeyed, returning a few moments later with the word :

"He is to be confined on board this vessel. You
lads are to go into the cabin."

We obeyed right willingly, for neither of us cared to remain while our prisoner was being taken on board, and having gone below into Captain Perry's cabin, we were called upon to give a detailed account of our forenoon's work.

When the story was finished my father sent us on deck again, neither he nor Alec's brother making any comment, and once there we saw that the traitor's boat was empty. He had been disposed of in some fashion which did not concern us, so that there was no possibility of his being able to carry further information to the enemy.

Old Silas, the gunner, met us near the companion-way, clasping each by the hand as he said, with more feeling than I had believed it possible for him to display : —

"You have done good work this day, lads, but unwittingly caused sorrow to many in Presque Isle; for there be no honest man who will feel other than deepest distress because of findin' a trusted neighbor to be a villain."

"Would it have pleased you better, Master Boyd, if we had let him go free?" Alec asked.

"Heaven forbid, lad! While one may be distressed because of the unmaskin', there'll be great relief at knowin' that information of our movements is no longer bein' sold to the enemy. I have no question but you have saved the fleet from destruction, unless it so be he has already carried word of our intention to take the vessels over the bar. Once the Britishers know that we count on leavin' the bay, you may be certain Captain Finnis's squadron will lay off an' on waitin' a chance to pounce upon us."

"What will they do with him?" I asked.

"That is more than I can say. He deserves the death of a traitor; but whether there be sufficient proof against him is another matter."

"Surely you do not believe there is any question of his purpose in being on the lake front where we found him?"

"Not a bit of it, lad; but what we believe is one thing, and legal proof quite another. Howsomever, there is no reason why we should spend our time talkin' of him, for it's a subject that gives one a bitter taste in the mouth. There is much work to be done on shore, an' we'd best take our share of it. While you lads were ferretin' out traitors, an hundred and five men arrived; therefore, as I have heard it said this mornin', Captain Perry has about three hundred officers an' men fit to do duty. A scanty number with which to man two twenty-gun brigs an' eight other crafts; but they are to be distributed around in the most economical fashion possible, an' we shall put to sea as soon as the fleet can be got over the bar."

"How long will that take?" Alec asked.

"I cannot say; but certain it is that we are to move down to the entrance of the harbor to-morrow mornin.'"

This was Saturday, the last day of July, and with the thought in my mind as to the breaking of one of the commandments, I asked old Silas if he believed it would be right that we should put to sea on Sunday.

"We are to make a move in the mornin', lad. War is a wicked thing at the best, an' those who engage in it give little heed to God's day, so that an advantage may be gained. Our commanders have the idea, from some information brought by General Mead, that no time is to be lost, and orders have already been given for the fleet to make ready. Even the small craft must be lightened in order to get them over the bar, and I understand that there is much doubt in Captain Perry's mind, as there is in my own, whether the *Lawrence* and *Niagara* can get out at all. It won't be a short job at the best, and I'm allowin' a week will be well nigh spent before the cruise is begun."

By the time the old man had finished speaking we

were in the traitor's boat, pulling toward the shipyard where the "camels," having been completed, were being tested.

It was dull work here for Alec and I, since there was little we could do to aid in the task, and I proposed that we spend the remainder of the day with my mother, for it might be many weeks before such another opportunity would be ours.

Therefore it was that until daybreak on Sunday morning, the first of August, we remained quietly at home, and then set out with my father, who had come ashore about midnight, to take our places on board the *Lawrence* as members of her crew.

Old Silas was there, ready for duty, as might have been expected, and when the brig, under the influence of the early morning breeze, passed the town toward that neck of sand which threatened to deprive us of the opportunity to take part in the battle we believed to be near at hand, every woman and child in the settlement stood on the shore to witness what they probably believed was a departure.

The cruise came to a speedy ending.

The *Lawrence* dropped anchor with her bow just resting on the sand-bar, and orders were given for the gunboat *Trippe*,[1] which was the smallest vessel in

---

[1] Formerly the *Contractor*.

the fleet, to go ahead for the purpose of ascertaining the depth of water.

When she grounded, not more than fifty yards from where the flag-ship lay, it seemed certain we would not be able to get a single craft out, and Alec Perry said despondently to me: —

"It seems as if we were fated to remain idle while the Britishers hold control of the lake. It were better my brother had remained at Newport, than to come here only to be balked of his purpose."

I could say nothing cheering, for the same thought was in' my own mind; but Captain Perry and my father were not men who could be so quickly disheartened. An obstacle in their way only served to arouse them to greater effort, and one would have said that this apparent disaster had long been foreseen and provided for.

The entire fleet had come to anchor when the gunboat grounded, and, as if by previous arrangement, every small boat near the shipyard and the shore round about put off to take part in the arduous labor which must be performed before our squadron could be gotten into deep water.

Now came five days of excessive and exhaustive labor, during which time I do not believe Captain Perry was below more than two hours on a stretch,

o

although Dr. Parsons had declared that he was dangerously ill, and then the work had been performed.

It is not seemly that such a task should be passed over in few words, and yet my story has run so long already that what these brave men did must be described in the smallest possible space.

The gunboat *Trippe*, in command of Lieutenant Smith, was the first craft over the bar, and the work of lightening had not been excessive. All which was taken from her could be cared for in small boats, therefore once she was in deep water her armament and stores were quickly on board again.

The *Porcupine*, commanded by Midshipman Senat, and the *Ohio*, captained by my father, went over at about the same time, that is to say, during Sunday night.

The *Scorpion*, with Sailing-Master Champlin in command, did not succeed in crossing until Monday noon, and it was late on that night before such goods as had been taken from her could be put on board again, since it became necessary to carry a goodly portion of them ashore.

The *Tigress*, with Master's Mate McDonald acting as captain, and the *Somers*, under Sailing-Master Almy, were gotten over before Tuesday noon.

Then came the *Caledonia*, with Purser McGrath in command; and the *Ariel*, captained by Lieutenant Packet, crossing on the evening of the third day.

There were left inside only the *Lawrence*, which Captain Perry himself commanded; and the *Niagara*, under Captain Elliott, to be carried over.

But these last were, as old Silas put it, "the tough nuts of the lot;" for if it was necessary to take so much from the smaller craft before they were sufficiently lightened, it did not seem possible that the two brigs could, even by aid of the camels, be forced into the waters of the lake.

All this while, as may be imagined, the strictest watch was kept, for we knew full well Commodore Barclay was somewhere in the vicinity with his squadron, and it stood to reason that he expected we would attempt such a manœuvre as was then in progress.

Immediately the smaller vessels had been forced into deep water their guns were put in position and loaded; everything was made ready as completely as if we knew an attack would be made within the next hour, and had the Britishers appeared while the brigs were comparatively helpless, I doubt not but that they would have met with a warm reception, although it is not reasonable to suppose we might have succeeded in beating them off.

When, on the morning of the fourth day, work was begun upon the *Lawrence* and *Niagara*, every man and boy among us was in a state of the greatest possible excitement. We understood full well how deplorable would be our plight if the enemy should appear just after the guns had been taken from the brigs, for then the two vessels on which we placed the greatest reliance could have had no part in the battle that must have ensued.

Right here let me set down what, as a matter of course, we could not know at the time; but which explains why we were allowed to perform this long task unmolested.

I have seen a letter which Mr. Ryason wrote to my father, and from it comes this extract: —

"The citizens of Port Dover, a small village on Ryason's Creek, a little below Long Point, offered Commodore Barclay and his officers a public dinner. While that dinner was being attended, Perry was getting his vessels over the bar, and thereby acquired power to skilfully dispute the supremacy of Lake Erie with the British. At the dinner Commodore Barclay remarked, in response to a complimentary toast, 'I expect to find the Yankee brigs hard and fast on the bar when I return, in which predicament it will be but a small job to destroy them.' Had Barclay been more mindful of duty, his expectations might have been realized."

If we of Presque Isle had had this information at the time, it would have saved us great distress of mind, for there was not among all our forces one who thought otherwise than did old Silas.

He said to me despondently, when the order was given to load into small boats the guns from the *Lawrence:* —

"Now has come the time, lad, when I believe of a verity that our ruin is near at hand. It does not stand to reason that the British commodore can hold off longer, for he knows full well we would set about crossing the bar at the earliest moment, and if he sights us at this work while the two brigs are dismantled, we are undone."

During the earlier portion of the task the men had labored with now and then a jest or a cheery word; some speculated as to what would be done once the ships were afloat, and all seemed in a certain degree happy, although excited. But now, when we were doing that which would compass our own destruction should the enemy's squadron heave in sight, every face wore an expression of deepest gravity; men spoke in whispers, as if fearing the lightest sound of their voices might be token of what we were about, and I saw no smile, nor heard an idle word during all that while.

To get the camels into position under the brig was a difficult matter, but finally accomplished, and on the morning of the 4th of August Captain Perry's flag-ship, with every small boat towing ahead, was hauled across the barrier of sand into the waters of Lake Erie.

Then, while a portion of the force labored at dismantling and making ready the *Niagara* for the same passage, the remainder set about replacing the guns, reloading the ammunition and the stores, and by two o'clock of that day every man and boy among us breathed more freely, for one of our ships was in condition to give battle to whosoever might attempt to work us a mischief.

By thus dividing the laboring force in order to arm the *Lawrence* as speedily as possible, the work on the *Niagara* required much more time than it had on the flag-ship, and not until noon of the 5th did the last vessel of the squadron move out over the bar.

Just at that moment, when our work was so well-nigh completed that we need have little fear, the enemy's squadron appeared in sight.

Commodore Barclay had at last come to his senses; but it was too late, so far as capturing the Yankee fleet on the bar was concerned.

Eight-and-forty hours previous, the sight of the British flags hoisted on vessels carrying forty-four guns would have filled us with dismay, and well it might, for then our doom was sealed.

Now, however, having successfully combated greater difficulties, we felt as if the coming of Commodore Barclay was something so trifling as not to be considered, and many of our people, like old Silas, rejoiced in the belief that we might even at this moment, when the *Niagara* was virtually dismantled, give them battle.

Among those who were eager to meet the British, even though we were unprepared, was Captain Perry.

It is proper now, perhaps, that I call him by a higher title, since he was really in command of the fleet, and I noted the fact, as did Alec, with most intense satisfaction, that once the vessels were in deep water the men spoke of our commander as "commodore," when previously it had been simply "captain."

We had a taste of what this young commander was ready to do, when he sent orders to Lieutenant Packet and Sailing-Master Champlin to go out with their respective vessels, the *Ariel* and the *Scorpion*, and boldly engage the squadron for the purpose of detaining them until we should be able to come up.

This order was so much to the liking of those who were sent to repeat it to the commanders of the schooners, that they shouted the words loudly that all might hear, and as we labored with redoubled efforts, although well nigh on the verge of exhaustion, to refit the *Niagara*, a shout of satisfaction and triumph went up such as must have been heard by the tardy Commodore Barclay.

"We are in for hot work now, lads, and plenty of it," old Silas said in a tone of satisfaction, as we two lads assisted him in mounting one of the guns that had just been sent on board, for every able-bodied man from the *Lawrence* had been ordered to aid in the work of refitting this last vessel to cross the bar. "Our commodore isn't one to shilly-shally 'round when there's a chance of burnin' powder with good effect, an' his sendin' the schooners out in such prompt fashion shows that he ain't minded to lose an opportunity for a fight."

"Think you there will be a battle this night?" Alec asked, so excited that his voice trembled.

"That is accordin' to yonder Britisher's stomach. If it so be he says the word, I'll warrant you we'll go with our three hundred men — hardly more than enough to work the fleet — and give him such a taste of our metal as won't be pleasin'."

"If Oliver should set out so poorly prepared and be whipped, the government would blame him as severely as if he had a full force," Alec said, half to himself;

and I understood from the words that the lad hoped Barclay was not of the mind to wait until we might come up with him.

"But he won't be whipped, lad;" and old Silas spoke in a tone of confidence, as if he could read the future. "We Yankees have been kept cooped up in Presque Isle bay so long that each will do the work of three men when the chance is given him. We'll not be whipped, lad, as Barclay shall soon learn to his cost."

Now it was that as we worked every one of us gazed seaward at brief intervals, looking with pride upon the little *Ariel* and *Scorpion*, while they stood boldly on toward the British squadron that could have sunk them with a single broadside, the stars and stripes flying proudly from their mastheads, and all hands doubtless at quarters, hoping it might be possible to engage in a contest, however unequal.

But the battle was not to be on that day, and well perhaps for our commodore that his challenge was not accepted, for the odds against us might have proven too great, despite the eagerness of the men.

Before the two schooners were come within range of the enemy's ships the squadron was put about, heading for the North Foreland, crowding on all sail as if it was feared our tiny schooners might insist upon a battle.

We cheered, as a matter of course, when the enemy thus fled, and laughed in derision at his cowardice; but there was beneath it all a deep disappointment because the time had not come when we might show our strength and determination.

"Never you mind, lad," old Silas said, as we stood looking after the retreating fleet, and doubtless showing in our faces signs of that which was in our hearts. "Never you mind. Commodore Perry ain't the one to hang 'round here while there's a British vessel afloat on Lake Erie, and I'm willin' to wager all my prize-money that if Commodore Barclay doesn't come out boldly to meet us, we shall hunt him up, and the battle won't be long delayed unless it so chances the gallant redcoats surrender without firing a gun."

CHAPTER XII.

AS a rule the crews of the several vessels shared the old gunner's opinion regarding Commodore Perry's intention of giving us all the work possible, now that his squadron was at liberty.

It seems really wonderful, as I look back on those days when I hoped to win fame as a soldier or sailor, how quickly the men came to have confidence in our boyish-looking commodore. Hardly one of them had ever seen him before he arrived in Presque Isle, and yet all were ready to trust their lives in his hands without reserve.

All believed as did old Silas, and every one labored with a will to make the *Niagara* ready that there might be no delay when our commander found the opportunity to strike a blow.

At five o'clock on that afternoon the last gun had been brought off from the shore, and without waiting until the decks could be put shipshape, word was passed from one craft to the other for all to make sail, following the lead of the flag-ship.

"Now you can see whether I told the truth," old Silas said triumphantly when the *Lawrence* was gotten under way, her flags floating proudly in the breeze. "There's not a craft in the fleet ready for action, and yet off we go in search of the enemy. Precious little time lost in that kind of work, eh?"

Nobody grumbled because of such eagerness, although it kept us all jumping mighty lively when we should have been bottling up sleep after four nights of almost incessant labor; but we toiled and sweated hour after hour as cheerfully as if it was done solely for our private benefit.

By break of day we had arrived off the North Foreland. The vessels were in something approaching proper trim, and half of. the men had been told off to take a watch below.

Alec and I were among those thus released from duty, yet we remained on deck when our eyes seemed glued together owing to lack of sleep, in the hope that we might catch a glimpse of Leon Marchand.

Although I have never mentioned the lad's name since relating the particulars of our second escape from North Foreland, I have not kept silence because we failed to think of him.

Hardly a day had passed but that we held converse regarding the French boy, speculating as to what might have been his fate after the soldiers discovered that he had led them on a wild-goose chase, and promising that whenever the fortunes of war should permit we would do our best at finding him.

Therefore it was we remained on deck when we might have been sleeping, even though there was not one chance in a thousand of seeing, or, if we did catch a glimpse of the lad, there could be no possibility of having speech with him.

We sighted no living thing along the entire shore of the North Foreland.

By aid of a glass it was possible to make out the barracks where the troops had been encamped; but they appeared to be deserted, and we had good reasons for believing that the famous descent upon Presque Isle was abandoned.

The British squadron was keeping out of sight also, and I, believing Commodore Perry would make immediate search for them, suddenly discovered cause for alarm.

"Suppose your brother sails either east or west with the hope of coming across Commodore Barclay, is he not leaving Presque Isle unprotected?" I asked of Alec, as if believing he could answer the question in a satisfactory manner. "Who shall say that the much-talked-of expedition is not near the town at this moment, having awaited just such an opportunity as has now been given?"

Old Silas passed at the moment I spoke, and, overhearing the question, took it upon himself to make reply: —

"Do you think our commander can be so stupid as you are tryin' to make out? I'll go bail that we look in at Presque Isle bay as often as once in every four-and-twenty hours so long as the wind serves, an' while it holds calm there's little chance the Britishers will land any very great shakes of an expedition."

"That's it, exactly!" Alec cried, apparently much relieved by this view of the matter. "I knew Oliver wouldn't leave his base of supplies at the mercy of the enemy, yet didn't see 'exactly how it might be guarded if we were to search for Commodore Barclay's squadron. There's no hope of our seeing the French lad, and we'd best take our trick below, Dicky Dobbins, before it expires."

"That's where you're right, lad!" the old gunner cried approvingly. "Never lose a chance to take a rest, and by such means you will always be ready for hot work."

Then we two lads went to our hammocks on the gun-deck, and, once stretched out at full length, slumber visited our eyelids with but little delay.

We were not awakened until sunset, and then going on deck we saw dead ahead, hardly more than two miles away, the entrance to Presque Isle bay.

Old Silas was in the right when he said we should look in here as often as once in every four-and-twenty hours, for until the 9th day of August we cruised back and forth, watching and praying for a sight of the enemy.

It was on the morning of the fourth day since our fleet came out across the bar, that we received reliable intelligence concerning the enemy from a French-Canadian, who was friendly to the Americans because of his enmity to the British.

Commodore Barclay had gone with his squadron to Malden, there to await the completion of another ship which was nearly ready for sea, and it was generally believed he would remain in that harbor until able to strengthen his fleet by the addition of this new craft.

It seemed that he was unwilling to meet us on equal terms, although having professed eagerness to come at us in any shape, regardless of men or armament, and now had gone into hiding until he might have nearly two guns for every one of ours.

On the strength of this information General Mead decided to disband the militia which had come to the defence of Presque Isle. The larger number of them were farmers, and it was high time they got into their harvest fields.

Therefore, on this 9th of August the troops marched out of the town, and once more the citizens banded together in military fashion to protect their homes.

This day was destined to bring great changes and decided advantages to all of us, whether ashore or afloat.

The militia had hardly more than gotten out of the town before an hundred disciplined sailors and marines, well officered and under command of Captain Jesse D. Elliott, marched in, and immediately signals were set in token that those on shore desired to communicate with the commander of the fleet.

It can well be fancied that we were overjoyed by the arrival of this sadly needed reënforcement, and the squadron came to anchor just off the bar to receive the newcomers.

The men and officers already on the *Niagara* were distributed among the other vessels, and the brig was put under command of Captain Elliott, who took on board with him the force he had brought in.

Commodore Perry now had under his command nearly four hundred men, and the moment had come when he believed it his duty to report as being ready to coöperate with General Harrison, even though by so doing he would be leaving Presque Isle at the mercy of the enemy.

"I'm allowin' Barclay won't have a chance to do much mischief in this section of the country," old Silas said, when a dozen or more in the watch to which we two lads belonged were discussing the news that had been whispered around, no one knowing how it had leaked out of the cabin. "Our commodore ain't countin' on givin' the Britishers any very great amount of spare time, an' that famous squadron of theirs will have to move mighty lively in order to steer clear of a row."

To me it seemed almost wicked, this going away from Presque Isle when it appeared as if the town was in greatest danger; but Alec argued that in war there can be no discrimination, and that, as in all things, "the greatest good to the largest number" is the rule to be observed.

It made little difference, however, what I might have thought of this new order of affairs. The command was given that the fleet make sail for Put-in-Bay, and the town wherein was my mother must be left with no other protection than could be afforded by the armed citizens.

If Captain Elliott had arrived twelve hours earlier, or if General Mead had delayed an equal length of time before disbanding the militia, the situation of

P

affairs might have been far different, and my heart would have been less heavy on that morning when we set sail in regular battle order to begin active operations against our country's enemies.

During such time as we were at sea nothing in the way of a British craft was sighted, and now is the moment when I may set down certain matters regarding the traitor Alec and I had captured.

Until this morning when we left the entrance of Presque Isle bay, some of us never to return, I had believed Nathaniel Hubbard was confined on board the *Caledonia;* but as we made sail I heard one of the sailors complaining that he was deprived of what might be a last glimpse of home in order to "feed a villanous traitor."

"Who is it?" I asked, surprised at learning there was any one imprisoned on board the *Lawrence.*

"You should know, seeing that you had a hand in his capture," the man replied surlily. "Why he wasn't sent on shore instead of bein' transferred to this brig, beats me."

"When was he brought aboard?"

"The night after we crossed the bar, and before the fleet put across to the North Foreland."

"Are we to carry him with us on this cruise?"

"You'll have to ask the commodore for that infor-

mation.   I'm not supposed to know what he counts
on doin'.   It's enough for me that I must fetch an'
carry for a gallows-bird like him."

The man was in such an ill temper that it was
useless to question him further, and I went to old
Silas, as both Alec and I had come to believe was
our right.

It was plain to be seen, when I put the first question, that Master Boyd could give much more information than he then seemed disposed to do.

He answered me almost curtly, never volunteering
even an opinion, and this was so entirely contrary to
his usual manner that my suspicions were aroused.

"It seems to me that Alec and I have the right to
know what is being done with the man," I said hotly.
"We captured him without aid from any one, and yet
it is forbidden us to know other than that he was put
on board the *Caledonia*."

"There's no call to lose your temper, lad, seein's how
the fellow has been held just as you delivered him,
except that a change of prisons was made, and I'm
allowin' the commodore ran away with the idea that
he might venture thus far without your permission."

I was ashamed, immediately after having spoken,
and the old man's reply only served to increase my
confusion.

"It is proving myself a simple, to speak in such a tone," I said humbly. "There's no reason why either Alec or I should know anything regarding the prisoner which the commander wishes to keep a secret."

"From what I've heard and can guess, I allow you two lads will not have the chance to complain of bein' kept in the dark, so far as he's concerned, many days longer."

"What do you mean?" I asked, my curiosity provoked by his air of mystery.

"Time will show, and you're young enough to be willin' to wait a few hours."

Having said this, old Silas turned away, as if his breath was too valuable to be wasted on one like me, and I went in search of Alec.

He was in the commodore's cabin, one of the officers told me, and I, not daring to venture there without special invitation, was forced to curb my impatience as best I might.

An hour later, when I had heartily repented having spoken so hastily to old Silas, a sailor came with an order for me to present myself before the commander in his quarters.

"The gunner has repeated what I said, and now I must confess myself a meddling fool before the one man above all others whose good opinion I wish to keep," I muttered to myself while obeying the order, and when I finally stood in the presence of the commodore the expression on his face frightened me.

He looked as grave as if about to pronounce sentence of death, and Alec, who sat on a locker near the bunk, was pale and nervous.

"Surely," I said to myself, "there is no good reason for their making so much ado about the words I spoke thoughtlessly;" for it seemed to me that I had been summoned solely because of what I said to old Silas.

"Richard, did you know that Nathaniel Hubbard was a prisoner on board this brig?" Commodore Perry asked abruptly.

"Silas Boyd told me, when I was so foolish as to question him."

"You must also understand that we cannot in justice take him into action, and it is certain we shall engage the enemy before many days have passed."

I nodded my head like any simple, wondering what connection there was between such a proposition and my hasty words.

"You and my brother made a prisoner of the man, and thereby performed most valuable service, because if he had carried to the enemy information of what we were about to do, it is probable the fleet would not have gotten across the bar without a scratch."

Again I nodded, and thinking now of that inter-view, I can well understand what an idiot I must have appeared.

"Because of the great service you performed, and also since I believe both you lads may be trusted implicitly, Captain Dobbins and myself decided, before getting under way, that you were the only two who should be allowed to know the outcome of the affair. The man deserves death, for I have no doubt but that he has played the spy upon the people of Presque Isle these many days, but it is an open question if he could be convicted of the dastardly crime, owing to lack of proof. Then, again, your father, Richard, is most eager to save an old neigh-bor and former friend."

The commodore paused for an instant, as if at loss for a word, and I looked in amazement at Alec, who sat on the locker, gazing first at his brother and then at me; but it was impossible to read any solution to the seeming mystery upon his face. He answered my glance without a change of expression, and I fancied he was questioning me with his eyes.

"Captain Dobbins and myself have decided that no good can come of trying to punish the traitor, while by showing mercy — mistaken mercy, perhaps, — he yet has an opportunity to redeem himself.

Therefore it is that we take you lads into our confidence, asking your assistance."

I was even more bewildered than before, and gazed in open-mouthed astonishment at my commander.

"We depend upon you to liberate this man as secretly as may be, trusting only Silas Boyd, who will lend the necessary assistance, and allow it to be believed that he escaped."

For a moment it seemed to me I must be dreaming! I could not believe that my father, whom I knew was devoted to his country, and Commodore Perry, who had been literally consumed with impatience because he could not come at our enemies, would plot to release a traitor — a man ready to sell his friends and his native land to the highest bidder.

"I see that the proposition astonishes you, as it did Alexander; but it is a sound one, of which I am not ashamed. Talk the matter over with my brother, and by the time the plans can be put into execution you lads will have come to a thorough understanding concerning it."

Having said this the commodore arose, a movement which I understood to be a token that the interview was at an end, and as I turned to leave the cabin Alec linked his arm in mine, walking in this fashion until we were come on deck, where I observed old Silas gazing at us curiously.

Not until we were well forward on the forecastle-deck where none could creep up on us unawares, did I speak, and then it was to ask : —

"What do you think, Alec Perry, of this proposition to set free a traitor who would have delivered us over to the enemy without remorse?"

"It has the approval of both your father and my brother."

"Now you are begging the question. I asked for your opinion."

"At first I looked at the matter much as I believe you do; but after thinking it over, and I have had ample time, I fancy there is much of good in it."

"In what way?"

It would be impossible for me to set down here all the arguments Alec advanced in favor of the plan, explaining as he spoke that he but repeated what his brother had said. It is enough if I give the chief points, and it appears to me that the case should be made plain lest we be blamed for what we afterward did.

First the difficulty of proving the man's guilt was brought up, and I was free to admit that argument a good one, because we had really seen nothing which would absolutely fasten the crime upon him.

Then came the supposition that, being given a chance to redeem himself, Nathaniel Hubbard might become a better man. If he would do his part in such a plan it was strong reason why he should be set free; but I doubted the man's desire for reformation.

The shame which would come upon his family with the publication of his guilt was another argument, and I did not try to answer it. The strongest reason for freeing him was a general one, and did more toward convincing me than any other. I knew full well there were many in the United States who cried out that this was an unjust war — that Americans had no right to uphold it, and once it was noised about that a prominent citizen of the town which had begged the hardest for troops was in full sympathy with England, it would go far toward proving to the people at large that the wrongs of us on the frontier were imaginary rather than real.

I know not, even now the words are written, whether I have made my meaning plain; but it is the best I can do in the way of explanation. I know for a certainty that the arguments convinced me even against my will, and when we two lads came down from the forecastle-deck I was pledged to do whatsoever lay in my power to set Nathaniel Hubbard free in such a manner that the crew of the *Lawrence*, and all others in the fleet, for that matter, should remain in ignorance of our movements.

"When is it to be done?" I asked, as we walked aft, and Alec replied in a whisper: —

"After we have arrived at Put-in-Bay. There we shall come to anchor, and ample time will be given us."

This was the ending to our conversation, and the matter was not referred to again until the evening of August 15th, when our fleet entered the harbor known as Put-in-Bay.

Then it was that Alec said to me, when our duties were come to an end for the day, and we free to remain on deck or below as best pleased us: —

"The work must be done to-night. I will speak privately with my brother, and do you broach the subject to old Silas. We shall need the assistance of at least one man, and Oliver believes the gunner can be fully trusted."

Having said this Alec went into the commodore's cabin, and I approached Master Boyd, who was pacing the forward deck in a manner which told that he had some weighty subject for thought.

"I would have speech with you, if it so be you are at liberty," I began; and before it was possible to say more the old man interrupted gruffly:—

"Very well, lad; but there's little need to make many words over it, for I can guess what you would talk about. It goes mightily agin the grain to help such as that traitor; but I suppose it must be done if both the commodore and your father have set their hearts upon it."

"How did you know what had been kept a profound secret?" I asked in surprise, forgetting for the moment that the old man had intimated as much a few moments before the plan was revealed to me.

"Your father, fearin' lest I mightn't take kindly to the job, gave me a hint of what would be done, an' there's no likelier spot than this in which to work the traverse. I'll run the boat alongside near about midnight, an' you two lads must attend to the rest of the work."

Having said this much old Silas walked away, as if unwilling to speak further on a disagreeable subject, and I sat on the rail aft, feeling more anger against Nathaniel Hubbard because it was he who forced us to such work, than for what he may have done against his country.

Alec did not remain long below; in less than half

an hour he was by my side, holding up what I soon saw was a key.

"With this we can unlock the door of his prison. He is confined amidships in the petty officers' quarters."

"How are we to get him out secretly?"

"That is for us to decide. My brother will aid us so far as may be possible; but he must not take the chances of being known in the business. What does old Silas say?"

"No more than that he'll have a boat alongside at midnight. That is to be the extent of his work, as I understand it."

"How can it be done?" Alec said, half to himself, and it was beyond me to answer the question.

In silence we two sat on the rail with eyes fixed upon the deck, trying to puzzle out what would have perplexed older heads than were on our shoulders.

CHAPTER XIII.

IT lacked half an hour of midnight when I saw dimly in the gloom the outlines of a man in a boat on the port side of the brig, and knew that old Silas had fulfilled his promise.

Alec and I had moved restlessly to and fro during the evening, sometimes walking together, and again separating for a time, as if courting loneliness; but without having arrived at any decision regarding a method by which the traitor could be secretly released.

We had formed plans in plenty; but on discussing them some fatal defect was presented, and midnight was like to find us still undecided as to how the work might be performed.

"We will trust to chances," Alec said finally, after old Silas had made his boat fast and clambered up on the brig's rail, where he seated himself. "It is not possible to figure out every detail beyond liability of failure, and we can only hold ourselves in readiness for whatever may happen."

This was not an unwise speech in view of the fact that we had racked our brains in vain during four hours or more, and it was with a most profound sense of relief that I gave over the mental effort.

"Is it all arranged?" the old gunner asked in a hoarse whisper, when I passed near where he was sitting.

"We have agreed upon nothing," I replied. "At the last moment matters may turn in our favor."

"Does the traitor know what we are figuring on?"

"I suppose Alec's brother has given him a hint of how matters stand."

"Why not lounge around below, and see how the land lays?"

"Look here, Master Boyd," I said, seized by a sudden idea, "why should you not take this matter in hand? You can make a success where we would meet only with failure."

"I'm not minded to dirty my hands more than is necessary," the old man replied emphatically. "If traitors are to be turned loose instead of hanged, let some one else work the traverse."

There was little thought in my mind that I might be able to convince Silas Boyd it was his duty to help us yet further than had been promised; but, having nothing better to do, I set about the task, and by virtue

of soft words, mingled with much flattery, I finally succeeded so far that he said, as if angry because of having yielded : —

"I'll make a try for it, lad, though it's hard lines
when a man at my time of life sets about lendin' traitors a helpin' hand. Get into the boat, an' see that
Alec is with you, for if it so be I succeed, we'll need
to get away in a hurry."

Then the old gunner went below, and I walked
aft where my comrade was standing near the head
of the companionway, hoping, most likely, that his
brother might come on deck to offer some sugges-
tion.

An exclamation of relief and joy burst from his
lips when I repeated what had passed between Master
Boyd and myself, and it can readily be fancied that
we lost no time in taking our places in the little
craft, which had been borrowed from one of the gunboats, as I afterward learned.

During fully an hour we remained silent and motionless, alternately hoping old Silas would succeed,
and fearing lest he had been discovered, and then
two dark forms appeared on the rail above us.

I would have called aloud in order to make certain
who they were, but that Alec prevented any such in-
discretion by placing his hand firmly over my mouth,

and while I was thus powerless to speak the gunner and the traitor descended.

Old Silas cast off the painter, giving the light skiff a vigorous push which sent her far away from the brig's side, and when we were swallowed up by the gloom Alec and I plied the oars.

"Where shall we land?" my comrade asked, when we were midway between the brig and the shore.

"It makes little difference," Master Boyd replied sulkily, as if angry with himself because of having taken part in such business. "So that we gain the mainland, one place is as good as another."

No other word was spoken until the skiff's bow grated upon the sand, and our prisoner arose to his feet. Then he said in a low tone, his voice trembling with suppressed emotion : —

"I shall never forget what has been done this night. The word of one like me is not counted for much by those who hold true to their country, yet I ask you to believe it. I have come to realize fully the enormity of my crime, although until taken prisoner I believed myself justified in the course pursued. From this moment it shall be my earnest endeavor to repair the wrongs committed against my countrymen."

Having said this he stepped ashore, and an instant later was lost to view in the gloom.

"Perhaps it is best he should go free," Alec said with a long-drawn sigh of relief, and old Silas replied in an angry tone : —

"We have made ourselves akin to him by this night's work, and I shall never have the same respect for myself that I had four-and-twenty hours ago."

Then he took up the oars, pulling vigorously toward the brig, and after a brief interval I made bold to ask : —

"How did you succeed in getting him off?"

"It was a simple matter. The sentry went forward to light his pipe; and, with the key you gave me, the door was soon opened. Hubbard must have been warned of what would happen, for he came forward immediately, and I had but to lead the way after having locked the cabin as before. We met no one while coming aft, and soon it was so dark that those on deck might have rubbed elbows with us and not known who walked by my side."

"It is well over, and I feel as if a great load had been lifted from my shoulders," Alec exclaimed.

"With me it is as if a heavy burden had been put on my back," old Silas added. "The business is done, so far as concerns settin' the traitor free; but now we stand a chance of this night's work bein' known to our messmates, in which case not one of 'em would so

Q

much as look at us again. There'll be a hue an' cry when it's known he's no longer aboard, an' there's a good show of our bein' suspected."

This last possibility did not trouble either Alec or I as it did the old man, and we went on board the brig with the belief that the disagreeable matter was finally ended.

We turned in quietly, as may well be imagined, but I had not gained any great amount of sleep when I was awakened by a tumult on deck.

"Hubbard's escape has been discovered," Alec whispered when I sprang up, so bewildered for the instant that I failed to understand the meaning of the noise. "Our best plan is to remain here as if yet asleep."

As he suggested, so we did, and after a short time the confusion subsided; when, despite the gravity of the situation, slumber again closed my eyelids.

It was broad day when I awakened; Alec was standing by the side of my hammock, and the report he made was most assuring.

"I have just been on deck. Matters there are in our favor; it is believed that the key was left in Hubbard's door by the marine who served him with supper — "

"That can easily be disproven by finding the key."

"It has been kept in the mess-room, in charge of the third officer, who now reports it missing. In my opinion, old Silas got hold of it after coming aboard last night. At all events, there appears to be little fear of our being suspected, more particularly since we shall put to sea again as soon as a fresh supply of water can be taken aboard."

Although the escape of a prisoner through what appeared to be carelessness on the part of his keepers was a serious matter, it sank into insignificance when a sail was sighted three miles off the entrance of the harbor, and signals were set for the *Scorpion* to put off in pursuit.

The schooner was quickly gotten under way, and while this was being done orders were given for the entire fleet to follow.

In less than ten minutes after the lookout had reported the stranger, our squadron was carrying full sail, the *Scorpion* leading by half a mile or more, and every man laboring under the greatest excitement, for it surely appeared as if we were in a fair way to make a prize.

The escape of the traitor was entirely forgotten, for the time being, and we lads knew full well that the commodore would not press the matter unless it should seem necessary in order to avoid suspicion.

Most exciting was this chase after we made out beyond doubt that the strange sail was a British vessel heavily armed.

Every stitch of canvas was spread, and the question as to which craft in the fleet was the best sailer bid fair to be settled before we were come up with the chase.

The Britisher was a clipper, and soon gave evidence that she could hold her own against our swiftest vessel; but where there were so many against one it seemed almost certain we might succeed in cornering her.

I venture to say that every man aboard the *Lawrence*, including the commodore himself, remained on deck during the entire day, watching the chase eagerly.

Now and then it would seem as if the *Scorpion*, which craft was by long odds the swiftest of the fleet, gained on the stranger, and our hopes rose accordingly; but only to be dashed a short time later when the Britisher recovered her lost ground, darting ahead at such a pace as threatened to give her an advantage that could not be overcome.

The chase headed for the Canadian shore on first discovering our squadron; but, fearing most likely that we might cut her off on the west and east, she soon hauled around on a course directly up the lake.

Then, when our vessels were strung out in a line, she came about, actually doubling on us until headed for the North Foreland.

Signals were set for the fleet to make for the Canadian shore, and we were no more than on a new course when the stranger hauled around once more, this time making directly for Put-in-Bay.

"She counts on givin' us the slip among the islands," old Silas said late in the day, when it was certain the Britisher could not safely make another turn, because orders had been given for our vessels to take such a course as would cut her off from any more twisting and turning.

"She's lost, once she gets inshore," Alec replied gleefully. "We should be able to hem her in with but little trouble, and I warrant that Oliver isn't losing the sight of such a possibility."

"He may have such a plan in mind, but I misdoubt his being able to carry it out," the gunner said, as he scanned the horizon. "Unless this is the time when all signs fail, we'll soon have so much wind that it will be a question of shortening canvas, and the commodore won't be so venturesome as to fool around among these islands, takin' the chances of losin' one or more of the fleet."

Until this moment I had failed to note the unpleasant fact that the wind was rising rapidly.

Low-hanging clouds in the east told of a storm, accompanied by more of a breeze than would be comfortable or pleasant, and, in addition, night was close at hand.

"The Britisher is in as much danger of coming to grief as we are," Alec said at length, after observing the signs of which I have spoken. "Our pilot should know the channels as well as theirs, and—"

An exclamation of dismay from Master Boyd's lips checked his speech, and, following the direction of the gunner's outstretched hand, we saw the gallant little *Scorpion* come to a sudden stop, roll to and fro for an instant, after which she settled down in such manner as told us she had taken ground.

An instant later her canvas was furled, and we knew that, so far as she was concerned, the chase had come to an end.

The Britisher had disappeared behind Put-in-Bay island, and she was no more than shut out from our view when the squall burst upon us with a fury such as I have seldom seen equalled.

It surely seemed as if the elements conspired to aid our enemies, and at that moment I lost hope.

Commodore Perry was a man who appeared to gain courage when the outlook was most gloomy, and now he gave new proof of his ability to command.

Signals were set for the fleet to heave to, and when this had been done, the first officer was sent to each vessel with instructions as to where they should anchor.

The night had fully come before these orders could be obeyed, and then, from the location of the riding-lights, we could see that each craft had been stationed where she might best guard the outlet from the islands.

Unless the Britisher had put to sea during the first outburst of the tempest, she was held prisoner, and we might make her our prize when the day dawned.

Master Champlin had already sent word that his schooner was resting easily on the sands, and could readily be hauled off when the wind abated, therefore we no longer had any anxiety concerning the *Scorpion*.

As may be supposed, every vessel in the squadron was snugged down in proper shape to ride out the gale, which promised to be as short-lived as it was fierce, and but for the fact that we had lost our prize there would have been nothing to disturb us.

The stars were shining brightly at midnight; the wind was no heavier than a gentle breeze, and every man in the fleet remained on the lookout for the Britisher.

Before morning the *Scorpion* was floated, and her captain reported that she had sustained no injury.

When the day broke every craft was under sail,

and within an hour we discovered that the enemy had given us the slip.

He must have gone out from behind the island in the teeth of the wind, while we were occupied with the *Scorpion*, and the first opportunity was lost.

"It's a bad sign," old Silas said, with an ominous shake of the head, when we had discovered that the Britisher was not within our grasp. "It's a bad sign, an' I'd be willin' to give up all the wages comin' to me on this cruise if it hadn't happened."

"Don't croak, Master Boyd," Alec shouted, with a hearty laugh that went far toward driving the sense of disappointment from my heart; "signs don't count except among old women, and because we failed to capture one small Britisher, there's no reason to believe we shan't bag plenty of them before this voyage has come to an end."

The gunner refused to be cheered, and as our fleet stood out from the harbor, heading for Sandusky bay, where General Harrison was encamped, Silas went below, as if there was no longer any necessity for him to perform a seaman's duty.

I am overly long in coming to that portion of my story which is of importance, and therefore must put an end to the words lest it become necessary to cut short the account of that day when Oliver Perry made his name famous, at the same time giving every man of us an opportunity to distinguish himself.

We arrived off the point of the peninsula at the entrance of Sandusky bay on the morning of August 18th, and there signal guns were fired that General Harrison might have knowledge of our position.

Then we waited for some word from the troops until evening, when Colonel Gaines, with several officers and a guard of Indians, came on board.

Camp Seneca was only twenty-seven miles away, so the colonel informed our commodore, and boats were sent at once to bring the general out to the *Lawrence*.

Four-and-twenty hours later Harrison came on board with a large following of Americans and Indians, and for a time the deck of the *Lawrence* was much like a fair-ground.

From this time until a full week had passed, it seemed as if Silas Boyd was in the right when he declared that our failure to capture the first of the enemy's vessels sighted was proof that ill-luck would attend the cruise.

Immediately after General Harrison came on board plans for the campaign were laid, and we spent much time sailing to and fro to find a suitable place for a rendezvous.

Then my father was sent in the *Ohio* to procure additional stores from Presque Isle, and also to make certain that matters there were as they should be. At the same time the fleet sailed toward Malden on a reconnoissance, but was met by heavy weather which rendered it impossible to accomplish anything of importance.

While off the mouth of the Detroit river, Commodore Perry, Dr. Parsons, Alec, myself, and fully forty others, were attacked by what was called "bilious fever," and so many were on sick leave that it became necessary to make some port.

On the 27th of August the squadron came to anchor in Put-in-Bay harbor, and instead of being war vessels, it was much as if ours was a fleet of floating hospitals.

Alec and I were quartered aft, greatly to old Silas's displeasure, for he held that we should have remained with our messmates; and a most dismal time we had of it.

The doctor was so ill that it was necessary he should be carried from one bedside to another, else had we received no medical attendance, and we were forced to get along without nursing, waiting upon ourselves as best we might.

Four days after coming to anchor, General Harrison sent thirty-six men to act as marines, and take the places of those sailors who were too feeble to even stand watch.

With a view to giving the invalids a needed tonic, Commodore Perry ordered the squadron under way, and we cruised to and fro, where I know not, for at the time I was so ill as to give no heed whatsoever to anything around me.

It was the 5th day of September when I had recovered sufficiently to go on deck, — Alec left his bunk four-and-twenty hours before it was possible for me to move about, — and then many of the crew were convinced that within a few days at the most we would have an opportunity to engage the enemy.

I believe of a verity that such intelligence did more toward reviving the invalids than any of the nauseous potions Dr. Parsons forced them to swallow, for within twenty hours every man had shown himself on deck, eager to learn what might be the prospects for a fight.

Old Silas was the one to whom we lads applied for information, as may readily be guessed, and that which he told us was in the highest degree cheering.

Our scouts had ventured into Malden, and there learned beyond question that the enemy were on the point of making a move in some direction.

It was said that General Proctor's army had but a

scanty store of provisions, and it had been decided Commodore Barclay should at all hazards open communication with Long Point, where were gathered the British supplies.

Our commodore believed this information to be true, as could be understood by the precautions he was taking to prevent the enemy from slipping past him.

Lookouts were stationed on Gibraltar island; every vessel was kept in readiness for a quick start; anchors were hove short, sails only loosely stowed, and no man, save those who acted as watchmen, was allowed ashore.

We could be in sailing trim within five minutes after the Britishers hove in sight, and, weak though the majority of the men were from the recent attack of fever, we knew full well all hands would give the red-coats a good sample of how Yankees could fight.

Each hour brought us nearer the battle in which we believed we should win some honor for ourselves, and inflict considerable injury upon the foe, and it was said by his messmates that old Silas slept with one eye open, lest by closing both at the same moment he might lose time in opening them.

It is impossible for me to give even a faint idea of the suppressed excitement under which we labored during these long, weary days of waiting!

Fancy what a strain it must be on the nerves to know

for five days and nights on a stretch that at any moment one might be summoned to do desperate battle for his country — that he might meet his death during the engagement, or at the best come out maimed for life, and some slight idea can be had of our mental condition from the hour of learning that it had become absolutely necessary for the British commodore to leave his hiding-place.

On the evening of September 9th, all the officers of the fleet were on board the *Lawrence*, having been summoned by the commander to a consultation for the purpose of deciding whether it might not be wise to attack the enemy's squadron even while it was under the guns of the fortifications at Malden.

The gentlemen were on the quarterdeck, and amidships the crew had gathered, hoping to catch a word now and then which would give them an idea of what might be expected.

Then it was that our commodore did that which would have endeared himself to every man in his command, even had he been unfriendly with them up to that time.

Alec and I were sitting cross-legged on the deck by Master Boyd's side, and, thanks to the light of the full moon, could see everything that took place aft.

The officers had been excitedly discussing the question of attacking Commodore Barclay while his vessels remained at anchor, when Alec's brother suddenly unrolled a square, blue banner, on which in letters formed of white cotton, were the words uttered by the gallant commander of the *Chesapeake:* —

"DON'T GIVE UP THE SHIP."

"There, gentlemen," he said, holding the bunting high in the air that all might see it, "there is the flag under which we will go into action, whether on the open lake, or in the harbor of Malden. When this flag is hoisted at the mainroyal masthead, it shall be your signal for opening the engagement. We will meet Commodore Barclay inside of four-and-twenty hours, and when that long-hoped-for moment comes, remember the instructions Nelson gave: 'If you can lay your enemy close alongside, you cannot be out of your place.'"

When he ceased speaking every man of us leaped to his feet as if moved by a spring, and what a round of cheers rent the air!

It was a timely vent for the excitement which had kept us in a fever so long, and we yelled until those on the other vessels hailed to know what had set us going.

If I could have been in Commodore Perry's stead, and heard an hundred men or more cheering me in that fashion, it would have been glory enough for one lifetime.

SAIL HO!

ALTHOUGH we — and I mean the crew — had no assurance that our fleet would soon engage the enemy, every man appeared to be positive a battle was near at hand.

The unfurling of that blue banner appeared a promise to be fulfilled in the near future, and when the excitement had in a measure died away we began discussing the probable result, no one venturing to suggest that the Britishers might possibly come off best. Victory seemed assured, despite the fact that Commodore Barclay carried thirty-five long guns to our fifteen; we said to ourselves that Perry would soon lay us alongside the enemy, when our smaller pieces must equalize the weight of metal.

Why every man felt confident a battle was very near at hand, I am unable to say.

Beyond the fact that the officers had been discussing the advisability of attacking the enemy in Malden harbor, should he refuse to come out, there was nothing to indicate an immediate meeting with him, yet we spoke among ourselves as if a decisive engagement would positively be fought on the morrow.

Old Silas was the only man among the crew, with the exception of the officers, who had ever smelled burning powder in a fight on shipboard, and this night his opinion was eagerly sought for and implicitly relied upon.

"From what our commodore did at the taking of Fort George, I hold to it we shan't work at long range many minutes, if it so be the wind serves us properly," he said to the group of men around him, among which were Alec and I, and my comrade interrupted by saying proudly : —

"You may be certain of that! Oliver isn't one who will hang off when an enemy is within striking distance!"

The old gunner paid no attention to this remark, but continued, as soon as the lad ceased speaking : —

"Leftenant Forrest told me that our scouts have reported the Britishers' strength to be much in this 'ere way. The ship *Detroit*, just off the stocks, so to speak, carryin' nineteen guns, one in pivot, an' two howitzers ; the ship *Queen Charlotte*, with seventeen guns an' a howitzer ; the schooner *Lady Prevost* mountin' thirteen guns an' a howitzer ; the brig *Hunter*

R

of ten guns; the sloop *Little Belt*, carryin' three guns, an' the schooner *Chippewa*, with one gun an' two swivels. Now as you all know without my tellin' you, our strength is fifty-two guns an' two swivels. If Captain Dobbins were here with the *Ohio*, we'd be a little better off; but seein's he has gone to Presque Isle, it's a case of gettin' on without him, which is like to make his heart ache when we sail into the bay with a long string of prizes."

"My father would not have gone at such a time unless he had been ordered to do so," I said quickly, thinking for the moment that the gunner would have it understood differently.

" I know that full well, lad. There's no man in this fleet, or among the Britishers, for that matter, who doesn't know Daniel Dobbins for a brave sailor, to say nothin' of his bein' the best navigator on the lakes. As I said, his heart will ache when he hears that we've given the Britishers a lickin', an' he wasn't here to take a hand in the scrimmage."

" Accordin' to your own figgerin', we need a good sailin' breeze when the Englishmen heave in sight, else we're likely to be taken at a disadvantage," one of the sailors suggested.

" Right you are, lad, right you are; an' yet when they heave in sight there's like to be a stiffish breeze, else

Barclay would hold snug in port. Of course it'll be another matter in case we run into Malden after 'em."

"You've counted up only the guns, Silas," another sailor cried. "What about the men?"

"There's where we're a bit weak, I'll admit; but a Yankee who's fightin' within sight of home should be able to count for more than one Britisher. It's said Barclay has better than five hundred men, all in good condition — one hundred an' fifty from the royal navy, eighty Canadian sailors, two hundred and forty soldiers, mostly regulars, an' a sprinklin' of Indians. Now Leftenant Forrest tells me we've four hundred an' ninety names on the muster-roll; but one hundred an' sixteen are on the sick-list, an' nigh to all of that number too weak to lend a hand at anything. Therefore you can set our force down as three hundred an' seventy-five all told, one quarter bein' from Rhode Island, a quarter regular seamen, the third quarter green hands, an' the balance made up of niggers and Injuns."

"If that figgerin' be true, an' I'm not sayin' it ain't, the Britishers have about an hundred an' twenty-five the best of us," the sailor who had first spoken said gravely.

"That's the size of it, lad."

"Then what about its bein' our trick to fight at close quarters?"

"We're bound to do it with the idee of evenin' up the weight of metal. I'm not allowin' that the difference in men goes for very much, seein's how us Yankees are bound to do the most fightin', in consideration of bein' at home."

To my mind the old gunner's argument was not a good one; we knew full well that the Britishers were as brave as we, and a goodly number of them were near to their homes.

It pleased me that our men should be confident of winning a victory, and yet I feared for the result.

By thinking long on this subject I might have grown timorous while all the others were so brave; but I put the matter from my mind by saying that there were no more signs of an immediate battle than at almost any other time since we crossed the bar of Presque Isle bay, and for the moment I was near to wishing that Commodore Barclay might find it possible to give us the slip.

The crew of the *Lawrence* gave little heed to sleeping, on this night; there were a few who turned into their hammocks, but Alec and I were not among the number. It would have been impossible for me to close my eyes while death seemed so near, and he, dear lad, could not rest because of the anxiety in his heart.

We two left the group of sailors who listened eagerly to the wondrous tales with which old Silas was regaling them, and walked well aft where we might see the commodore when he came on deck, for the officers of the brig had gone below immediately after the new banner was displayed.

"If Oliver lives through the morrow, he will have won for himself a name such as few can boast of," Alec said proudly.

It seemed as if the lad lost sight of himself in the great love he bore this brother who was our commander, and, realizing that a trifling accident might change the fortunes of war, I said, with the idea of lessening his disappointment in case it chanced that the British won the victory : —

"We are the weaker in both guns and men, Alec, and old Silas argues idly when he claims that our people can fight better than the enemy."

"Commodore Barclay is not as good an officer as Oliver."

"He has surely had more experience," I ventured to suggest.

"That does not count against such a man as my brother."

"I am ready to admit all you claim for our commodore, and make even stronger statements; but yet it is not well to be so positive regarding the result, Alec dear. No man can say what a day may bring forth, and our crews are to be pitted against experienced men-of-war's-men."

"Oliver will be the victor!" the lad said emphatically, and in such a tone as told me that any attempt to make him less confident might cause hard feelings between us.

"God grant he be!" I replied, and never did I speak more fervently; the words were, in reality, a prayer. Then, coming back to the thought which had been near to a hope, I added, "We are counting on a battle to-morrow as if there could be no question about it, and yet what grounds have we for believing that the Britishers will venture out of Malden harbor?"

"Oliver says they will," Alec replied, and as against such profound faith I could say no more.

We paced to and fro until nearly daybreak, and then the commodore came on deck, looking weak and worn from the ravages of the fever; but with a sparkle of the eyes which I could see plainly even in the darkness.

He threw one arm around Alec's neck, and held out a hand for me to clasp.

"What are you two lads doing on deck at this

hour, when you should be in your hammocks gaining rest and strength against the work of this coming day?"

"Then you really believe we shall at last face the Britishers?" Alec asked, caressing his brother's hand.

"Ay, lad; for if Commodore Barclay refuses to come out, it is decided that we shall go in after him."

"And am I to serve on Master Boyd's gun, or will you permit that I stand by your side?"

"Remain at the station to which you have been assigned, dear lad. My choice would be to have you close by me; but every hand is needed, and I am certain you and Richard will count as men during the engagement."

I tried in vain to make a fitting reply, but the words refused to come when most needed, and it was possible only to press his hand warmly in token of my good intentions; yet at the same time there was a terrible fear in my heart lest at the critical moment I might show myself a coward.

"You can depend upon us both so long as we are alive," Alec said, in a tone so solemn that it was as if he had a premonition of sudden death.

"That is my true brother!" the commodore said proudly. "I have no question but that you will prove yourself worthy to be called Americans. Now

I beg that you seek repose. A brave man cares well for his body, lest it should be weaker than his will."

"Have you slept?" Alec asked quickly.

"It would be impossible; and, besides, the belief that we shall soon meet the enemy has so refreshed me that I no longer need rest."

"It would be useless for me to lie down, Oliver. How could I sleep when within a few hours my brother is to show the world that no braver man than he lives?"

"It is not well that praise be bestowed before having been earned, Alec dear," the commodore said, with a low laugh. "I promise to do my best; and after the victory has been won you shall say what you please."

Then we three paced to and fro on the quarter-deck, the commodore's arm yet around his brother's neck, and I holding him firmly by the hand, for in that hearty clasp I found much to give me courage.

It was in this fashion that the light of a new day found us, and I believe the marines, who paced to and fro guarding the commander's quarters, shortened their beats, lest by advancing too near they break in upon what was neither more nor less than a season of devotion.

As the light grew stronger, from this vessel and from that came signs of life, until the still air was vibrant with the hum of voices, and it seemed good to be alive.

I had, for the time being, forgotten that the day was come on which our people believed we would be brought yard-arm to yard-arm with the enemy, until startled almost into timorousness by a cry from the lookout : —

"Sail ho! Sail ho!"

It seemed in the highest degree improbable that the anticipations of our people were to be so soon realized, and yet I found myself, with many another, gazing out over the lake in the expectation of seeing our enemy coming toward us.

Nor were we disappointed.

The morning breeze was feeble and gave indications of soon dying away entirely, yet Commodore Barclay had at last left his place of refuge, driven out by lack of provisions, for there on the sparkling waters could be seen the British squadron heading west by south, making for the North Foreland in quest of the supplies which the king's army were needing.

In a twinkling, as it were, Commodore Perry forgot all else save that the fleet for which he had waited so long was in sight. Wresting himself free from us two lads, he was on the instant transformed from the loving brother and dear friend into the eager, valiant commander.

Hurriedly, speaking so quickly that one order was almost merged into the other, he gave the word for signals to be hoisted, and within three minutes from the time the lookout reported a sail, our bunting was flying.

"Enemy in sight!"

"Get under way!"

These commands were given by the tiny flags which floated from the *Lawrence*, and in a twinkling every vessel in the fleet was alive with hurrying, eager men, rushing here and there like unto a swarm of bees.

The premonitions of the previous night had not been vain; at last the enemy for which we searched was in full view, and now nothing save rank coward-ice could prevent an encounter.

I quaked inwardly, not because a battle was about to be fought, but lest while it was waging I should shame my father by proving myself a coward; and, in fact, I was near to being one at that moment, when it was shown we would have an opportunity of measuring strength with the foe.

Timid though I was, and fearing for myself, I yet

had enough of Yankee courage to weigh well the chances for or against us.

The wind was blowing light from the southwest, and on the horizon were low-hanging clouds which gave promise of rain. There was not weight enough in the breeze to admit of our manœuvring freely, and I wondered how it might be possible for the commodore to bring the fleet into close quarters, as old Silas had declared was necessary in order to equalize the weight of metal and force of men.

But even a coward must have been inspired by the scene around him. Here, there, and seemingly everywhere, were Yankee sailors making ready for the fray, and all working with an eagerness which told how fearful they were lest this opportunity, so long sought, should be lost.

The clanking of chains as the anchors were hove apeak; cries of the men as they cheered each other in the work which preceded the carnage; the shrill whistles of the boatswains as they thus repeated the orders given by the officers, and the beat of drums summoning men to the shedding of blood, would have aroused the most timorous, causing even a coward to feel a sense of pride that his countrymen were so willing to try conclusions with a foe that was superior in strength.

Alec and I hastened to our stations, even though knowing that many hours must elapse before the guns could be used, and there we found old Silas, as might confidently have been expected, overlooking all the details lest he should be caught napping.

"Well, lads, the Britishers have shown themselves at last!" he cried, when we came up. "I felt in my bones last night that the time was nigh at hand when we might show the king's men they had no right on these 'ere waters; but never counted on their comin' to the scratch so early. We've got plenty of time to give them a sound drubbin', 'twixt now an' sunset."

"There's time enough," Alec said, speaking carelessly, as if used to such work; "but how are we to get at them? There isn't weight enough in this wind to move the brig, save at a snail's pace."

"I'm allowin' that the commodore will find a way to give us the chance we want. Look at him now! If yonder fleet gets off without our havin' a fair show at 'em, it'll break his heart!"

"All that I agree to; but even my brother can't command the wind."

"He can do what will amount to the same thing, lad, and before nightfall you won't complain because we didn't burn our powder in proper fashion. Two or three boats' crews ahead with a tow-line will make this old hooker walk through the water as if the girls at home had hold of her."

"Do you fancy the Britishers will stand still while we're towing our fleet into position?" Alec asked with a laugh.

"Ay, lad; unless they're willin' to show the white feather in face of a weaker force. There's nothin' save the power of Him who rules all things, that can prevent a battle this day, so set to work an' get this 'ere piece into proper trim, for once we're lyin' yard-arm to yard-arm with Barclay's flag-ship there won't be much chance for cleanin' up."

I noted with no little surprise that all the men around me were eager for the coming battle. There were no loud boasts, but on every countenance could be read a desire to stand face to face with the enemy, and nowhere did I see any show of fear.

The men did not jest as was their wont; there was no shuffling around lazily, but each was on the alert, eager to do his full duty, and seemingly anxious lest something should be left undone that otherwise might work to give us the victory.

And that we would win the battle I believe every one was confident, although equally positive that much blood must be shed before the end was attained.

The bravest or the most cowardly knew beyond a

peradventure that e'er the day was come to an end many of them would be still in death, or suffering from horrible wounds, but yet all wore a smile of content.

It was enough that the British commodore had at last given them the opportunity of proving their metal.

While the bustle of the final preparations could be heard on every hand, the crews were piped to breakfast under orders from our commodore himself, for Oliver Perry was one who looked well after the comfort or well-being of every man in his command, however much he might abuse his own body.

Food would have choked me at that moment when death was so near at hand, staring in the face every individual member of the crew; but Alec made a hearty meal, and, as I now look back on the events of that day, I realize the fact that those who showed the most bravery ate the most heartily.

Old Silas behaved as if appetite increased with each succeeding mouthful, and whenever he took a sip from his hook-pot of tea, it was to drink a health to those who would lead us into the game of death.

"We're in rare luck!" he cried, when his breakfast was ended because the mess-kid had been emptied. "I ain't sayin' but what we deserve it, after chasin' all over Lake Erie to find the Britishers; but yet at the same time it's sheer luck to get them where there's no runnin' away from a fight, an' they shall have enough of it before this day has come to an end."

"You may be ended before the day is," a red-faced sailor cried, as if trying the courage of our gunner.

"An' supposin' I am, lad, what better endin' can an old shell-back like me ask for? So that the stars and stripes float over yonder fleet when the sun sets, it's enough. As against givin' England a proper lesson, my life don't amount to the snap of a finger! It will be a glorious way of gettin' out of this world."

While such conversation as this was being carried on, clouds obscured the sun's face, and the rain drove those of us who disliked a wetting between decks, for until this moment we had been where a view could be had of the enemy.

No one paid any particular attention to what gave promise of being only a shower, save that the wind might come with the water, and thus give the Britishers a chance to continue on toward the North Foreland, where they could fight under cover of their shore-batteries; but it still held reasonably calm.

In less than ten minutes the clouds had dispersed, and the weather-wise among us predicted that a breeze would soon follow.

"We shall get enough to take us out from among these islands, lads, and I venture to say it won't help Johnnie

Bull to any great extent!" old Silas cried gleefully. "All we need now is to have plenty of powder an' ball near at hand, for there'll be little time to travel from the gun to the magazine after our work is begun."

The British were indeed waiting patiently for us, or, at least, so it seemed to me, although Alec said, later in the day, they could not have done otherwise without writing themselves down the veriest cowards.

The enemy's fleet lay just off our anchorage, swinging to and fro as the wind veered, and we could hear the sound of drums and fifes calling the men to quarters.

Our crew gathered on deck again when the heaviest of the shower was over, and all could see Commodore Perry as he paced restlessly to and fro, watching for an opportunity to strike the long-deferred blow.

The breeze which had been predicted sprang up, but not with such strength as filled our sails; and after waiting anxiously fifteen minutes or more in the hope that it might be increased, Lieutenant Forrest gave the command which all hands were expecting: —

"Boats' crews to their stations! Clear away, and let fall! Work lively, lads, and we'll see what effect a white-ash breeze will have on the brigs! Move with a will, for the flag-ship must be the first to tackle yonder enemy!"

CHAPTER XV.

THE FIRST SHOT.

THERE is a fair excuse for me if I linger long over this battle, when we gave to the English king such a surprise as I'm thinking he never had before, for it was my first real experience in that bloody business known as warfare, and so decided a victory that I can well be pardoned for feeling proud, even though my share therein was the least among all the brave spirits by which I was so fortunate as to be surrounded.

I would give to all my shipmates the full meed of praise which they deserve, and yet must I fail in so doing because every man was a hero, and to speak particularly of one seemingly detracts from the others.

It is only possible to say that each did his duty, and, perhaps, with the exception of myself, there was never one in all our fleet who did not burn with a desire to show the enemy what could be done when the opportunity offered.

It was not until near to ten o'clock in the forenoon that there was sufficient weight in the wind to fill our sails, and during all that time of waiting, when every moment was like an hour, the brave fellows chafed at the delay even as a lion chafes at the bars which confine him.

The British squadron was as helpless as we, and lay full in our sight without power of movement.

It may be that those on board the enemy's ships were as eager to come at us as we were to be at their throats, but I questioned it, because they did not have so much at stake.

When the breeze was sufficiently strong to belly out the sails, the command was given as I have already set down, and the words were hardly spoken before the boats' crews were at their stations, every man rejoicing because the moment had arrived when he might do something, however slight, toward hastening the laggard movement.

Slowly our vessels moved out on the bosom of the lake, every craft propelled by boats, and as we advanced the breeze freshened until, when the fleet was within two miles of the enemy's squadron, the sails were filled sufficiently to admit of our depending upon them alone.

Alec and I were standing well aft, for we had not

been told off as the crew of a boat, when the commodore said to his sailing-master, Mr. Taylor : —

"When the men have been called in you may run to
leeward of the islands."

"Then you will be forced to engage the enemy to
leeward," the officer replied, and although I failed to
understand the meaning of the nautical terms, my pulse
was quickened by the reply : —

" I don't care whether it be to windward or to
leeward; they shall fight this day! "

Then the tiny balls of bunting were run up to the
masthead, ordering the other craft to " wear ship,"
but before this command could be obeyed the wind
suddenly shifted until it came out of the southeast,
from which point it was possible for us to keep what is
called the " weather-gauge."

" Now we've got 'em in proper shape! " I heard old
Silas exclaim, and straightway my spirits rose, for it
seemed at the moment as if we had secured some great
advantage, though I failed to understand what it
might be.

The crew cheered when our fleet, the *Lawrence* leading, stood out toward the enemy, a white foam showing
under the stem of every vessel, and we went to our
guns, which had long since been loaded with the utmost
care.

It must be admitted that the Britishers presented a noble sight as we bore down upon them. Their vessels, newly painted and with colors flying, hove to in order to meet us, and now the timorous among us, I being of the number, could understand that they were not averse to an encounter.

There had been a faint hope in my mind that Commodore Barclay would shun an engagement, but that was dispelled on observing the preparations made to meet us.

Nothing short of an interposition by divine Providence could prevent a battle; and my heart sank within me as I realized that very soon many of the eager men who manned the *Lawrence* would be still in death, or writhing under the surgeon's knife.

The arrangements made for the care of the wounded struck a cold chill to my heart. The ward-room had been cleared that it might be used as a cockpit, and here Dr. Parsons laid out bandages and knives until it seemed as if he expected the entire ship's company would soon be under his care.

Half a dozen of those on the sick-list had been told off as his assistants, and they stood around the hastily constructed tables as if eager to greet such as might need their aid.

In all the hours that followed there was nothing

more horrible than these preparations for the carving
and slashing of those who as yet were sound in limb
and body, save it might be when the decks of the
brig were wetted and strewn with sand.

I did not understand the meaning of this last work,
and asked old Silas for an explanation, whereupon
he replied, as if speaking of some trifling matter : —

"It won't be long, lad, before these 'ere white
planks will be slippery with the blood of them who
are now so eager to be at the Britishers, and it is
to soak up that same blood that the sand is strewn
around. Presently, when you have occasion to go
to port or starboard, you'll realize how necessary
that may be."

I drew away from the old man, sick at heart. Such
precaution caused me to be more timid than had all
the predictions and conjectures.

I had my fill of warfare even before the action
began.

As I afterward came to know, during the consultation of officers in the commodore's cabin on the night
previous it had been decided that when the engagement commenced each vessel in our fleet should attack some particular ship of the British squadron.
As for instance: The *Lawrence* was to engage the
Detroit ; the *Niagara*, the *Queen Charlotte ;* and in

such-like order, every craft selecting an antagonist somewhere near her own size. Therefore now, when the wind permitted of our line being formed, the *Niagara* led the way.

Our ship had been cleared for action some time before, and as the real advance was begun Commodore Perry ordered that the blue banner, with its inspiring words in white, be brought up from his cabin.

Holding it at arm's length that it might be plainly seen by every one on deck, the commander said, in words that look cold enough when set down in writing, but which thrilled all who heard, and caused my faint courage to increase until I almost longed for the combat : —

"The enemy, for which we have waited so long, is at last before us. You know we are slightly outclassed in guns and number of men ; but to such brave hearts as yours that is of no especial importance. We shall soon be within range, and I promise that this brig be laid as close alongside the *Detroit* as the wind will permit. It is not for me to urge upon you the importance of doing full duty this day. Your country and your honor demands that the enemy be whipped. It was agreed between the commanders of the other vessels that when this was run up it should be the signal for action. On it are writ-

"'AY, AY, SIR, HOIST IT!'"

ten the last words of Captain Lawrence, and I know full well you will heed them. They signify your desire to fight to the last plank. My brave lads, shall I hoist it?"

He would have been the veriest coward living who could not have shouted as heartily as did we all, my voice rising high as any one around me: —

"Ay, ay, sir; hoist it!"

The flag was bent on to the halliards, and as it rose steadily aloft our crew burst into a very hurricane of cheers, which were echoed by those on the vessels nearest, for by this time I warrant that every man in the fleet knew the meaning of that signal.

We saluted it again and again, and as the tumult of voices went up on the morning air, I seemed to see before me the commander of the *Chesapeake*, as he spoke the words which were to be our battle-cry.

From that moment I ceased to hope that the action could be avoided.

To manœuvre the fleet into position was a slow task, and the hour of noon came while we were yet beyond range of the enemy, whose vessels were moving here and there to prevent us from gaining any advantage.

Our commodore, mindful of the wants of others,

ordered that food be served, and I saw men munching bread, cheese, or meat, grumbling meanwhile because it was not exactly to their liking, who an hour later had departed from this earth for evermore.

As for me, I would as soon have eaten with the coffin of my dearest friend for a table, as to have eaten then; but Alec was stouter hearted, and took his rations with a relish which I envied.

"It's not well to fight on an empty stomach, lad!" old Silas cried, when he saw me turn away from the food, and I foolishly replied : —

"It can make little difference to him who falls whether his appetite be satisfied or not."

"True for you, lad; but some of us will be alive when this battle is ended by the haulin' down of the British flags, and they'll need be ready to clear the decks of those who are no longer to be counted on the ship's list."

That the others cheered these words only served to show me how heartless men may become after having learned the "art" of warfare, and I turned away with a sensation such as cannot well be described.

Now the line of battle was formed. The British flag-ship, supported by the schooner *Chippewa*, was in the lead. After her came the brig *Hunter;* then the

Queen Charlotte, commanded by Captain Finnis; flanked by the schooners *Lady Prevost* and *Little Belt*.

The *Lawrence* led our line, with the *Scorpion* and the *Ariel* on her left, and the *Caledonia* on the right. The orders were that these three craft should encounter the *Detroit*, *Hunter*, and *Chippewa*.

Next came the *Niagara*, with instructions to fight the *Queen Charlotte*, while the *Somers*, *Porcupine*, *Tigress*, and the *Trippe* were to engage with the *Lady Prevost* and the *Little Belt*.

We were yet a full mile and a half away, and it was close to noon when a bugle sounded on the deck of the *Detroit*, the bands on the several Britishers struck up the tune of "Rule Britannia," and a ball from the enemy's flag-ship came directly toward the *Lawrence*, but fell far short of its mark.

The first shot of the battle had been fired, and, seeing the iron missile cleaving the air in a direct line for us, I involuntarily shrank behind Alec, whereupon old Silas shouted: —

"None of that, lad! None of that! A shipmate's body is no protection, and you should be willin' to take your full dose!"

The laughter which was provoked by this remark caused my cheeks to burn with shame, and from that moment I stood firm, however great might have been the fear in my heart.

"Remember that every shot does not go where it is aimed," Alec whispered to me, hoping with the words to check my fears; and I replied with such firmness of voice as could be summoned just then : —

"It was more instinct than fear which caused the movement, dear lad, though God knows I am afraid."

"So are all of us," he replied, with a hearty grip of the hand; "and he who talks the loudest is trying the hardest to prevent it from being known."

It seemed as if the blood stood still in my veins as we continued to advance slowly amid a silence so profound that I could hear my own heart beat; and then a cry of fear burst from my lips as another shot came toward us, plowing its way through the brig's bulwarks with a mighty shower of splinters, but, fortunately, wounding no one.

There must have been others beside me who showed signs of fear at this first proof of what the enemy could do, for Commodore Perry shouted, while he stood a fair mark for the enemy : —

"Steady, boys! Steady! There's not likely to be much blood spilled by such gunnery as that!"

Our commander was wearing no uniform; clad only in the garb of a common sailor, with blue nankeen jacket and white duck trousers, he was none the less a commodore, and there was not a Britisher so dull who would not have singled him out as the man who directed all our movements.

We advanced without opening fire until each vessel of our fleet was nearly in the position marked out for her the night previous, and then we set the signal to open the action.

The first gun on the American side came from the *Scorpion*, as I knew full well because of having my eyes on the schooner at the time; then the *Ariel* discharged two of her short twelves, and an instant later old Silas began his work.

This last shot struck the *Detroit* just above the water-line, plowing its way through her hull with a splintering of timbers which told that much damage had been done.

What a cheer went up from our men at this moment!

I think the fact that we had succeeded in sending a shot fairly home caused me to forget the danger, for certain it is I ceased to be afraid, and remained keenly on the alert for all that was passing around me.

I saw the schooner *Trippe*, outsailed in the advance, fully two miles astern, and wondered vaguely how long it might be before she would be near enough to give an account of herself.

The *Scorpion* and the *Ariel* remained near at hand, doing good work as I could see, viewing the scene like one in a dream, and I also understood that the enemy's squadron was concentrating all its fire upon our brig.

It was as if to them there was no other vessel in the engagement save the one bearing our commodore's flag, and that once she was disabled the victory would be won.

Within ten minutes after the first shot was fired I knew full well why the decks had been wetted and covered with sand.

Already were the white timbers stained crimson with the blood of my shipmates; but I was in such mental condition of excitement as neither to know nor care who had fallen.

I understood that Alec was as yet unhurt, because he worked by my side, cheering when a shot struck the enemy, and soothing with kindly word some poor fellow of ours who had been mangled by British iron.

That the *Lawrence* was speedily getting the worst of the fight could be told even by a lad like myself, and I felt a certain sense of satisfaction when Commodore Perry shouted through a speaking trumpet to the craft nearest, which chanced to be the *Niagara :* —

"Pass the word for all hands to make sail and bear down on Barclay. Lay him close alongside at all hazards!"

Then, even above the roar of the guns, I heard the order transmitted from one craft to the other, until it seemed that every sailing-master in the fleet must have heard it; but to my surprise the *Niagara* hauled off slightly, instead of obeying the commands.

To my eyes the engagement had ceased to be a battle, but was become a slaughter.

On every hand were dead, dying, or wounded men, and four times within twice as many minutes had the crew of our gun been so thinned out that old Silas was forced to call for assistance.

Then it was, just at the moment he urged one of the new men who had been sent to assist us, to stand bravely up to his work, that the old man's hip was shattered by a grape-shot, and he fell like one dead across the breach of the gun.

"We must get him into the cockpit," Alec said to me, speaking as calmly as if this was but an incident which we had been anticipating. "Take him by the head, and move quickly, else he will bleed to death before Dr. Parsons has a chance at him!"

Numbed with horror, I obeyed; and as we carried the old hero across the deck a stream of blood marked our way, making such a trail that it seemed as if his veins must have been emptied before we had traversed half the short distance.

Once in the ward-room I understood in a single instant what might be the horrors of war, better than I could have done by remaining on deck the full day.

The scene in this place, which was separated from the terrible tumult above only by the deck-planking, was more horrible than can be described in mere words.

The groans, the prayers of the dying, and the bustling to and fro of the surgeon and his assistants, all combined to make a noise more terrifying than the roar of the guns and the crashing of timbers.

The hue of blood everywhere, the cutting of human flesh, or the probing of ghastly wounds, sickened me until never again can I be brought to believe that there is anything noble or grand in warfare.

Even as we laid old Silas, now unconscious from loss of blood, upon one of the rough tables whereon were shreds of flesh and fragments of bone, a shot came crashing into the brig's side, tearing a passage straight through this place of torment, and releasing from their misery two poor fellows who had suffered the tortures of the amputating knife.

One of the surgeon's assistants was wounded by the same shot, but Dr. Parsons gave his attention first to old Silas, and in answer to Alec's eager question replied :—

"The wound is not necessarily fatal, lad. On shore I would say the man had every chance for recovery; but, unfortunately, he cannot have here such care as is needed."

I would have lingered by the old gunner's side, for I had come to look upon him as a friend, and it cut me to the heart that he might go out of the world without a word of farewell; but Alec forced me to accompany him.

"We are needed on deck, and by loitering here may lay ourselves open to a charge of cowardice."

Heaven knows there was no desire in my mind to loiter in that horrible place! I had lingered only in the hope the old gunner might revive sufficiently to give me at least a last word.

When we came out of the cockpit dense clouds of pungent smoke hid everything from view; it was difficult to distinguish objects ten feet away on our own decks, and I was thankful for the obscurity.

I knew, however, that on every hand were the dead and the dying; that the brig which had looked so neat and trim less than an hour previous, was torn and splintered, every plank dyed crimson by the blood of the brave men who had defended her so nobly, and that all the ships of the enemy's squadron were pouring into her a deadly fire!

"Where is the *Niagara?*" I asked of Alec, shrieking the question in his ear, otherwise he might not have heard it amid that thunderous din, and from out of the smoke came the voice of a grievously wounded sailor : —

"The cowards are hanging back, even though they were the first to get the order for close action. When the smoke lifted a few minutes ago I saw the brig almost out of range, using her heavy guns as if at target practice."

Alec, uttering a cry of mingled sorrow and anger, ran aft, I keeping close at his heels, and he had no more than gained the quarterdeck when a splintered fragment of our starboard rail struck him on the shoulder, literally tearing the clothes from his back.

I sprang forward quickly, believing him to be wounded; but the commodore was ahead of me, and for an instant he ceased to observe what was going on around us in his anxiety for the lad.

"I'm not hurt, Oliver dear," Alec said with a smile; but the sudden pallor of his face told that the shock had been a severe one. "It's not the nearest call for a wound that I have had," he added, showing his hat, through which had passed two musket-balls.

"I don't ask you to be less brave, brother mine, for now is the time when every man must hold his life cheaply; but you should be sufficiently cautious not to expose yourself unnecessarily."

"I came to ask why the commander of the *Niagara* had not obeyed orders? It is said she lays at long range while we are so sorely pressed."

"I cannot answer your question, lad," the commodore replied bitterly. "Elliott is no coward, and yet he has given us but little support. Richard Dobbins, go forward and ascertain how much damage the *Lawrence* has sustained in that quarter."

I obeyed on the instant, forgetting all my fear and horror in the terrible thought that we were surely being worsted, else why had our commander spoken in so hopeless a tone.

Once forward of the foremast, and I did not get there without stumbling again and again over a dead or a wounded man, it was as if I had suddenly boarded a wreck.

Everything was carried away forward from the ₔafter portion of the forecastle-deck, and I was like to being pitched overboard as I pressed blindly along until coming upon the very edge of the shattered timbers.

T

I believe of a verity that a missile of some description struck this portion of the brig every five seconds, and but for the horror of the discovery my legs would have trembled beneath me in abject fear of death; whereas I utterly failed to realize the danger.

The *Lawrence* was little better than a wreck; it did not seem possible she could swim ten minutes longer, and I hastened back over that deck slippery with blood, despite the sand which had been strewn upon it, to make my doleful report.

I had but just gained the quarterdeck when a round shot struck the mainmast within three feet of my head, sending huge splinters flying in every direction, one of them hitting Alec Perry full in the breast.

I saw the dear lad fling up his hands convulsively, and then pitch forward upon the deck like one smitten by sudden death.

It was as if that terrible sight deprived me of all my senses save that of affection for him who had proven himself such a true comrade, and with a cry of despair I flung myself upon the deck by his side, heeding neither the danger to life, nor of defeat.

CHAPTER XVI.

THE BATTLE.

AFTER reading over what has been set down, I am afraid that I have made it appear much as if the commodore, old Silas, Alec, and myself were the only Americans present at the battle of Lake Erie.

That I have said too much regarding my own fears and hopes is positive, and in these last pages I will try to remedy the matter by speaking of the battle as I have heard old and experienced men, who were present, describe it, halting here only so long as may be necessary to explain that Alec Perry was not dangerously wounded.

Every one who saw him fall felt certain he had received his death-blow. During fully a moment the commodore was convinced of the same; but within a very short time after I flung myself down by his side, the dear lad revived sufficiently to speak, and the terrible load was lifted from my heart.

Alec was badly bruised, as indeed any one would likely be who had been struck twice by splinters, but the injuries were not serious, and he refused decidedly to present himself before Dr. Parsons, as I suggested and even urged.

While we two lay there, I trying to make out if my comrade was nigh to death, Lieutenant Yarnall came up, looking more ghastly than any man I had seen since the action began. His nose had been cut through by a splinter, and was swollen until it resembled a huge piece of liver rather than anything I can bring to mind. He was bleeding from several wounds, but his courage was in nowise injured.

"All the officers in my division have been cut down, sir, and I would like to have others," he said, saluting gravely as if on parade.

"I have no more to give you," the commodore replied, returning the salute. "You must endeavor to make out alone."

"Very well, sir," and the first officer of the *Lawrence* returned through that storm of cannon-balls and musket-bullets to his station as calmly as he might have done had we simply been firing a friendly salute.

Now here is a description of the battle from the beginning up to this time, as I have seen it written down by one who was more familiar with the details than I, for enshrouded in smoke, and a novice in such matters, I know no more than what happened immediately around me : —

"Perry [1] soon perceived that he was yet too far distant to damage the enemy materially, so he ordered word to be sent from vessel to vessel by trumpet for all to make sail, bear down upon Barclay, and engage in close combat.

"The order was transmitted by Captain Elliott, who was the second in command, but he failed to obey it himself. His vessel was a fast sailer, and his men were the best in the squadron, but he kept at a distance from the enemy, and continued firing his long guns.

"Perry, meanwhile, pressed on with the *Lawrence*, accompanied by the *Scorpion*, *Ariel*, and *Caledonia*; and at meridian exactly, when he supposed he was near enough for execution with his carronades, he opened the first division of his battery on the starboard side of the *Detroit*. His balls fell short, while his antagonist and her consorts poured upon the *Lawrence* a heavy storm of round shot from their long guns, still leaving the *Scorpion* and *Ariel* almost unnoticed.

"The *Caledonia*, meanwhile, engaged with the *Hunter*, but the *Niagara* kept at a respectful distance from the *Queen Charlotte*, and gave that vessel an opportunity to go to the assistance of the *Detroit*. She passed the *Hunter*, and, placing herself astern

---

[1] Lossing's "War of 1812."

of the *Detroit*, opened heavily upon the *Lawrence*, now, at a quarter past twelve, only musket-shot distance from her chief antagonist.

"For two hours the gallant Perry and his devoted ship bore the brunt of the battle with twice his force, aided only by the schooners on his weather bow and some feeble shots from the distant *Caledonia*, when she could spare time from her adversary, the *Hunter*. During that tempest of war his vessel was terribly shattered. Her rigging was nearly all shot away; her sails were torn in shreds; her spars were battered into splinters; her guns were dismounted; and she lay upon the waters almost a helpless wreck.

"The carnage on her deck had been terrible. Out of one hundred and three sound men that composed her officers and crew when she went into action, twenty-two were slain and sixty-one were wounded. Perry's little brother had been struck down by a splinter at his side, but soon recovered. . . .

"While the *Lawrence* was being thus terribly smitten, officers and crew were anxiously wondering why the *Niagara* — the swift, stanch, well-manned *Niagara* — kept aloof, not only from her prescribed antagonist, the *Queen Charlotte*, now battling the *Lawrence*, but the other assailants of the flag-ship. Her commander himself had passed the order for close conflict, yet he kept far away; and when afterward censured, he pleaded, in justification of his course, his perfect obedience to the original order to keep at 'half cable length behind the *Caledonia* on the line.' It may be said that his orders to fight the *Queen Charlotte*, who had left *her* line and gone into the thickest of the fight with the *Lawrence* and her supporting schooners, were quite as imperative, and that it was his duty to follow. This he did not do until the guns of the *Lawrence* became silent, and no signals were displayed by, nor special orders came from Perry. These significant tokens of dissolution doubtless made Elliott believe that the commodore was slain, and he himself had become the chief commander of the squadron.

"He then hailed the *Caledonia*, and ordered Lieutenant Turner to leave the line and bear down upon the *Hunter* for close conflict, giving the *Niagara* a chance to pass for the relief of the *Lawrence*. The gallant Turner instantly obeyed, and the *Caledonia* fought her adversary nobly. The *Niagara* spread her canvas before a freshening breeze that had just sprung up; but, instead of going to the relief of the *Lawrence*, thus silently pleading for protection, she bore away toward the head of the enemy's squadron, passing the American flag-ship to the windward, and leaving her exposed to the still galling fire of the enemy, because, as was alleged in extenuation of this apparent violation of the rules of naval warfare and the claims of humanity, both squadrons had caught the breeze and moved forward, and left the crippled vessel floating astern."

It was only by the cessation of the shocks which told of the brig's having been struck by a ball that we on board knew the enemy was moving forward, leaving us little else than a hulk upon the waters.

Then the smoke of battle which had hung over our decks like a shroud was wafted away by the wind; and we saw the *Niagara*, half a mile or more on the larboard beam, engaged with the *Queen Charlotte*, *Lady Prevost*, and *Hunter*.

It was as if we had been cast aside as worthless, and that the remainder of the fight would be between those who had suffered less injury.

Perhaps, under another commander, such would have been the case; but Oliver Perry was never one to be cast aside or to shrink from any danger, and it was not in his mind to remain at a distance.

First, however, he gave heed to the gallant fellows who had been disabled; and Alec and I walked by his side as he moved from one to another of those who as yet had not been carried into the dismantled cockpit.

There were but fourteen men and boys on board who had not been injured more or less severely, and among them no more than two guns' crews could have been made up.

While we were amidships, Alec and I took advantage of the opportunity to run into the ward-room, where Dr. Parsons, now working alone because all his assistants had been summoned on deck to aid in working the brig, was performing his cruel-looking offices of mercy.

It was for the purpose of learning if old Silas yet lived that we ventured into the horrible place, strewn here and there with dismembered limbs or fragments of human flesh, and to our great joy the gunner had so far recovered from his faintness as to be quarrelling with the surgeon because that officer refused to allow him to go on deck.

"A bit knocked up, lads; but with blood enough left in my veins to give the Britishers another chance at drawin' it. This 'ere sawbones is takin' too much on himself, when he sets up that Silas Boyd shan't do his duty."

"There is nothing left for you to do, Master Boyd," Alec said, as he laid his hand upon the old man's head. "The *Lawrence* is out of the fight just now, and even though she wasn't, I question if you could find a serviceable gun aboard."

"You're not tellin' me that the brig has struck her colors?" and the old man would have sprung up but that we two lads held him down by main strength.

"Not a bit of it. The blue flag is still flying; but the brig appears to be little better than a wreck, and both squadrons have drawn off from us."

"And the fight? What kind of a turn is that takin'?"

"We appear to be holding our own."

"No more? No more than holdin' our own, lad?"

"I cannot see that we gain any advantage; but the flag-ship is the only craft which has been so badly used."

The commodore's voice from above summoned us to the deck, and as we clambered up the narrow companionway I heard old Silas giving the surgeon a tongue-lashing because the latter had threatened to tie the gunner to a stanchion if he persisted in his attempts to leave the cockpit.

When Alec and I were come on deck again an exclamation of surprise burst from our lips.

We had left the commodore clad in the garb of a sailor, smoke-begrimed and covered with the blood of others to whom he had lent a helping hand.

Now he was arrayed in the uniform of an officer in the American navy, from the epaulets to the sword, and looked to my eye more like a victor than one whose ship had been literally torn to pieces beneath his feet.

I stared at him in astonishment; but Alec, going to his brother's side, asked in surprise : —

"What is the meaning of this, Oliver?"

"Of what, lad?"

"Why have you laid aside the clothes you wore in action?"

"It is well that not only my own men, but the enemy, shall recognize me when I transfer my flag."

Alec looked at the commodore in mute surprise, and for the moment I believed our commander had lost his head.

"The *Niagara* appears to be in good condition," Perry said with a smile, "and it is from her deck that I will direct the battle to a glorious ending."

I looked out over the waters, which were literally boiling and spouting under the falling shot, asking myself how it might be possible for the commodore to do as he had said, knowing full well that the *Lawrence*, wreck as she was, could not be manœuvred.

"Lieutenant Yarnall," Perry said, turning to the first officer, who was bleeding from four or five wounds, with his face disfigured as I have already related, "I leave the *Lawrence* in your charge, with discretionary powers. Hold out, or surrender, as your judgment and

the circumstances shall dictate.   Have a boat lowered,
and detail a full complement of oarsmen, if it so be that
number of unwounded men be found aboard.   Take
down my pennant and the blue banner, for the remainder of the fleet shall fight under both until victory is
brought out of this tangle."

"Will you leave me here, Oliver?" Alec asked, when
Lieutenant Yarnall had set about obeying the orders.

"You shall go with me, lad, for it is well we two remain together while it be possible."

"And Richard?" the dear lad asked, noting the look
of entreaty in my eyes.

"He had best stay here; we cannot take too many
into such peril, for it will be no child's play to pull
through yonder storm of shot."

"You need oarsmen, sir, and I question if enough
can be found to man the boat, without taking every
one from the brig," I said quickly, distressed beyond
measure at the thought that I might be separated from
my comrade.

"You shall go as a member of the boat's crew," the
commodore replied promptly, and at the same time
kindly; "yet I am not certain it is a friendly act to
take you two lads through that deadly fire."

"We would venture very much more, sir, for the sake
of being with you," I made bold to say, and was re-

warded for the speech by a kindly smile from the man who on that day proved himself to be chief of a band wherein every man was a hero.

At this point Lieutenant Yarnall reported that the required number of unwounded men could not be mustered in the brig unless all the guns were abandoned, and I stepped forward, for now was come the time when I could make no claim of comradeship — in this hour of death the brothers stood apart by themselves, out of my world, as it were.

"With this lad, I can give you four at the oars, sir," the lieutenant reported, and our commodore replied, with that smile which had come to be in my eyes more precious than anything he could bestow : —

"It will do, Mr. Yarnall. The smaller the number the less to be put in jeopardy of their lives. Is the boat away?"

"Ay, sir, all is ready, now that the lad will be taken on as an able seaman."

Obeying a gesture of the lieutenant's, I went forward to the starboard rail, beneath which was the tiny craft for the conveyance of the commander-in-chief, and without venturing to presume upon any possible claims of comradeship, took my place among the oarsmen.

As soon thereafter as might be, the commodore and

Alec came over the shattered rail, the former carrying under his arm the broad banner of blue, and the pennant.

I had been eager to accompany the commander, and yet when I took my station in the boat, and had a better view of that stretch of water whereon it seemed that every square inch was covered by bullet or ball, the chance of escaping with life seemed less than when we stood on the deck of the *Lawrence* exposed to the fire of the Britishers' heaviest guns.

"Little show of takin' a cockle-shell like this across yonder stretch, eh?" one of the seamen said, with a grin, observing the direction of my glance, and most likely noting the sudden pallor of my face.

"It surely seems as if we would be cut to pieces before going fifty yards from the brig's side," I replied, and certain am I that my voice trembled like a coward's, although at the moment I was not conscious of what might rightly be called fear.

"That's what I allow will happen," the man said, as he stuffed his mouth full of tobacco. "It's a likely spot in which to swamp a boat, yet I'm not so sure but that a decent man would choose to die there, rather than in yonder hole where Dr. Parsons hacks an' hews to his heart's content before the breath of life goes out."

Perhaps it was some such reminder as this which I needed to give me the proper amount of spirit, for once he spoke of the cockpit I felt such a sense of relief at being free from it for the moment that there came to me a certain degree of calmness, enabling me to greet our commander properly when he came over the rail, followed by Alec.

It was as if my comrade shared in the glory which Commodore Perry had already won, and yet I did not envy him the honor. He was a brave lad, while I could be counted only as a timorous being whose courage was like to fail him at the supreme moment, and I felt more pride in his distinction of place than if our positions had been reversed.

Alec and his brother took their places in the stern-sheets, and the latter cried to Lieutenant Yarnall and the other bleeding, brave fellows who overhung the rail : —

"Do as you will with the *Lawrence*, Mr. Yarnall, and whatever may be the turn of affairs, count on our speedily coming to your assistance."

"God bless you, commodore!" was the gallant officer's reply, and then we left him on a sinking ship with only grievously wounded men as shipmates and crew.

It was the commodore himself who gave the order

for us to push off, and, as if thinking we at the oars needed heartening lest we should falter in the task after reaching that spot where the iron hail was thickest, he wrapped the pennant around his shoulders, standing erect while we pulled out to what seemed certain death.

Once we were clear of the brig it was as if the enemy knew full well the precious cargo our boat carried, and understood that only by compassing the commodore's death could they hope to win the day, for on the instant every gun was aimed at us, and every sharp-shooter on the Britishers' decks used us as a target.

I may live to be a very old man, and take part in many another battle, but it is not possible I shall ever again find myself in such a deadly shower as was poured upon us from the moment we left the side of the shattered *Lawrence*.

The bullets struck everywhere around us; the cannon-balls made the water boil and spout so high as to come over the gunwales until the light craft was in great danger of being swamped; but, singularly enough, not one found lodgment among us.

At that moment I believed a divine Providence was watching over our commodore lest he should come to harm, and I have never since had good reason to change my opinion.

Of a verity all the marines who wore red coats aimed their guns at Perry, and we at the oars cried out to him that he must take such shelter as was possible.

"It is proper the commander of a squadron show himself," was all the reply our entreaties could provoke, and finally I said to Alec, emboldened now by the despair which came upon me with the thought that the day was indeed lost if that bold spirit continued to present himself as a mark for the British bullets:—

"Unless the commodore sits down, and takes care to hide himself from sight of the enemy, I for one will lay down my oar, trusting that the wind may blow us out of musket-shot range!"

"I stand by what the lad has said," one of the seamen cried, and on the instant every man stopped rowing, for there was not one aboard minded to have any share in a martyr's death.

"To your oars, lads, to your oars!" the commodore cried excitedly. "Every second may be of the greatest value to us now!"

I had not the courage to oppose his will, but the eldest of the seamen said decidedly:—

"We're not warranted in disobeying orders, sir; but I for one will never carry you to certain death, whatever may be the commission you hold."

And another added:—

U

"Cease to make yourself so conspicuous, sir, an' you shall see how readily we will obey the lightest order you choose to give, even though knowin' we go to our death. It is your life, not ours, which is of importance this day."

The gallant young officer looked at us for an instant as if minded to administer some sharp reproof, and then I, who observed him closely, saw the moisture gathering in his eyes as he said in a low tone:—

"You be brave lads, all; and at such a moment as this there shall be no question of authority."

Whereat he seated himself by Alec's side, and the dear lad clasped his brother's neck closely as he looked at me with pride beaming from his eyes.

The bunting was unwound from around the hero's shoulders, and while he presented quite as fair a target for the bullets, it did not seem to us that he offered the enemy as much of an advantage.

Then we bent ourselves to the oars once more, pulling with every ounce of strength that could be forced from our muscles, and heading straight toward the *Niagara* whereon was Captain Elliott, hugging to his heart the belief that at last he was the sole commander of the American squadron.

It is not for such as me to criticise the doings of one whom the government had placed high in command, yet I say now, as I have a thousand times since that terrible yet glorious day, that the commander of the *Niagara* kept aloof from the heat of battle with no other idea in his mind save that he might rise to fame over the dead body of our commodore.

To look back now in my mind's eye on what I saw then, it seems like relating the story of some miracle to say that we came out of that murderous fire, pulling alongside the *Niagara* in safety.

Our boat was literally riddled with bullets, and yet not one of us had received a wound. Every oar was shattered, but we worked with such timber as remained, until our hero had been put in a position which enabled him to win the day.

Even now, the proudest memory of mine is that I did my share in winning the battle of Lake Erie, timorous lad though I am.

It was Captain Elliott himself who met Commodore Perry at the *Niagara's* gangway, and he stared as if facing a ghost, when our commander saluted him ceremoniously, for he believed him dead.

"How is the day going, sir?" Elliott asked, as soon as he could control his voice sufficiently to speak.

"Badly, Mr. Elliott, badly. I have lost nearly all my men; the *Lawrence* is a wreck, and I am transferring my flag and the banner to this ship. What are the gunboats doing so far astern? Why do they not bear their full share of the burden?"

"With your permission I will go to ascertain the reason, and bring them up."

"Very well, sir. Lose no time, and see to it that they come to close quarters without delay."

Then we, who had come out of death, as it were, clambered up on the *Niagara's* deck, cheered to the echo by every man who saw us, and the officer who for a few moments had believed himself first in command, took Commodore Perry's place in the stern-sheets of the boat with a full crew at the oars to carry him rearward.

CHAPTER XVII.

VICTORY.

TO men who had come from such a scene of ruin as had we, the *Niagara* appeared to be in perfect condition. But few of her crew were wounded, and she was in as perfect order for the conflict as if having just come from the navy-yard.

Before I could clamber up on her deck, being, as a matter of course, some distance behind Alec and his brother, the commodore's pennant had been displayed, and with it was run up the blue banner which bore the letters in white, and I venture to say that the death of the gallant Lawrence was fresh in the mind of every American on Lake Erie this 10th day of September in the year of grace 1813.

It was some such signal as this which our brave fellows aboard the other vessels needed to assure them that the commander in whom they trusted was still directing the course of events, and as the two bits of bunting were run up we heard a volley of cheers from every craft in the line, telling that the courage of all was strengthened.

"Now we shall win the day," Alec said confidently, as for a moment I came to his side, although, strictly speaking, my place was forward of the quarter, while he, released from duty as a member of the gun's crew under old Silas, had liberty to remain by the side of the commodore. "Now we shall win the day, for it is as if we were come into action with a fresh vessel, thanks to the timorousness of Captain Elliott."

Even as he spoke, and as if to check the exultation which had come upon us all when the commodore's flag was safely transferred, we saw the stars and stripes drop slowly down from the masthead of the *Lawrence*, in token that she had surrendered.

Dr. Parsons has since told me that when Lieutenant Yarnall, after consulting with Lieutenant Forrest and Sailing-Master Taylor, decided to show signs of submission, those poor wounded wretches in the cockpit, mangled and hacked until some of them no longer had the semblance of humanity, begged that the ship be sunk rather than surrendered, and refused to allow the surgeon to attend to their wounds, hoping they might die before the Britishers could take possession of the craft which had been fought so gallantly, yet so vainly.

However, it was not long that they were forced to remain thus hopeless.

Once our young commander had beneath him a craft which could be manœuvred, he changed his plan of action so far as the situation seemed to require, hoisting a signal once more for close action as the *Niagara* was steered straight toward the British line of battle, half a mile away.

As he had fought the *Lawrence*, so did he count on fighting her sister ship, and, inspirited by what they had seen, every man aboard our fleet was ready to follow at his beck wherever he might lead.

We had seen sharp fighting before; but now was come the time, as it seemed to me, when we were to take part in such an action as would dim all previous efforts, and even amid the noise and confusion of the conflict I found myself wishing that Silas Boyd might be with us, to have a share in the glorious dash which I knew was near at hand.

Now, indeed, was gone from my mind all sensations of fear. I ceased to have any thought of self, but lived only with those around me, making their fate as much a part of mine as if we were linked together in body, as in purpose.

Having come on board a vessel which had suffered comparatively small loss during the two hours of conflict, and, as has been said, was the best manned in the fleet, there was little Alec and I could do save to jump here or there, wherever a spare hand was needed, and set our shoulders to whatsoever portion of the wheel needed uplifting.

Therefore it was we had more of an opportunity to observe the battle. We could see, when the clouds of smoke were not too dense, each particular vessel, and knew, almost as well as did the commodore himself, what was taking place on the bosom of that lake whose waters, it seemed to me, should by this time have been stained crimson by the blood of brave men.

If I have made it appear that, up to this time, we two lads had seen the most desperate portion of the conflict, my purpose has been overrun, for once on board the *Niagara* the action became so fierce and deadly as to make it seem that until now we had been outside the range of the deadliest fire.

With the new flag-ship in the lead, and the signals for every craft to use both sails and oars so that they close in more quickly, we went straight forward toward the enemy, passing within half a pistol-shot distance of the *Lady Prevost* and the *Chippewa* on the larboard hand, and the *Detroit*, *Queen Charlotte*, and *Hunter* on the starboard.

We broke directly through the enemy's line, and not until we were come within such short range that I could have tossed my hat aboard either vessel, did we open fire.

Then it was that both broadsides were discharged; the *Niagara* rolled to and fro under the shock of the heavy guns, until it seemed as if every timber would be riven asunder; and from either side poured in upon us a cross firing, until a perfect network of whistling shot and bullets was formed above our heads, but fortunately so high that we suffered comparàtively little loss of life.

Here and there men fell, pierced by a musket-shot, or literally cut asunder by the heavy cannon-balls; but it was not as we had known it on the deck of the *Lawrence*, when nearly four-fifths of our people were disabled.

The din was fearful. One ceased to think of the loss of life, because in that terrific uproar it seemed only natural men must die.

The hue of blood which stained the white planking and the black bulwarks was no longer an ominous color, because that was needed to make the picture of war more perfect; and I believe every person on board the *Niagara*, save the commodore himself, lost, as I did, all thought of self in that pandemonium of destruction.

Right and left came broadsides from double-shotted guns; here, there, and everywhere poured in musket-balls from sharpshooters, who, in their excitement, had ceased to take aim.

Spars fell from aloft, or crashed on either side as our balls tore them from their fastenings on the enemy's ships; there were shouts of anger, cries of pain, moans and imprecations, while over all could be heard the crackle of musketry and the roar of heavy guns that was like to burst one's ear-drums.

It was no longer war, but had become a fever of death, wherein each man strove to kill, and regarded not his own life.

I would that some worthier hand could set down clearly the varied and rapidly-passing sensations which floated through my brain, for then might it be possible to describe to another what one experiences at such a time.

As for myself, I no longer thought of country or of the enemy. There was simply an intense desire to kill; an eagerness to see blood flow — for the time being we were become as brutes.

I know, because of having been told at a later day, that we passed straight through the British line; broke it, and, ranging ahead on the other side, rounded to, pouring great broadsides of hot iron into the *Detroit* and the *Queen Charlotte*, which vessels had fouled each other and were lying at our mercy.

I have since read the following description of what we did when I was no longer capable of seeing, or, seeing, was so overcome by feverish excitement as not to be conscious of that which lay fair before my eyes :[1] —

" Ranging ahead of the vessels on the starboard, Perry rounded to and raked the *Detroit* and *Queen Charlotte*. Close and deadly was his fire upon them with great guns and musketry. Meanwhile the *Lawrence*, having drifted out of her place in the line, her position against the *Detroit* was taken by the *Caledonia ;* the latter's place in line, as opposed to the *Hunter*, was occupied by the *Trippe*, the two vessels being commanded by Captain Turner and Lieutenant Holdup. These gallant young officers had exchanged signals to board the *Detroit* when they saw the *Niagara* with the commodore's pennant bearing down to break the British line. Turner followed closely with the *Caledonia ;* but the freshening breeze having brought up the *Somers* under Mr. Almy, the *Tigress*, under Lieutenant Concklin, and the *Porcupine*, under Acting-Master Senat, the whole American squadron, excepting the *Lawrence*, was for the first time engaged in the conflict. The fight was terrible for a few minutes, and the combatants were completely enveloped in smoke."

How long we were engaged after all the ships,

<hr>

[1] Lossing's " War of 1812."

save the poor wounded *Lawrence*, were brought into the conflict, I cannot say; so far as my own knowledge is concerned, it might have been five minutes, or as many hours, for I ceased to exist as a distinct human being; but had become simply a fraction, wherein the whole was the crew of the *Niagara*.

It so chanced that when the cloud of smoke lifted so that we might be able to distinguish objects at a distance, Alec Perry was standing by my side, having come forward with some order for his brother, and at that instant the British flag-ship, the *Detroit*, was lying plainly within our range of vision.

"We have at least given *her* a lesson!" Alec said, pointing to the shattered spars and fragments of rigging that had been cut by our shot, and even as we looked the British ensign was lowered from the masthead, fluttering in the breeze as it came nearer and nearer the deck, until I distinctly saw one of the seamen gather it up in his arms.

During an instant the full significance of this act escaped me. I stood, with my arm linked in Alec's, wondering what it all meant, when a great cheer rose from round about us, echoed by the crews of all the other vessels near at hand.

Then we knew that the *Detroit*, like the *Lawrence*, was out of the fight.

"We have whipped one of them!" Alec cried in glee, clapping his blood-stained hands childishly. "Commodore Barclay's ship has given up the fight, and now we shall see if he has pluck enough to transfer his flag in the heat of battle, as did my brother!"

At that instant, and when the crew of every gun was working with feverish haste to reload that they might take advantage of this first sign of submission, there came from the quarterdeck the command, loud, triumphant, and cheery: —

"Hold your fire, lads! The enemy is whipped!"

I wondered that our commodore could be so sanguine, for it seemed to me the Britishers would not admit themselves beaten until every craft was disabled; but, involuntarily glancing toward the right, I saw the cross of St. George being lowered from the masthead of the *Queen Charlotte*, and almost before I could call Alec's attention to the fact, every vessel in all that squadron, excepting the *Little Belt* and the *Chippewa*, were showing the same signs of submission.

It seemed incredible that we should have won the fight after having suffered such loss as had been inflicted upon the *Lawrence*.

It was impossible for the moment to believe that

this British squadron, whose commander had claimed he need only "come out and show himself in order to send the Yankees to their knees," had surrendered to a force much smaller than his own, and without discipline!

Even when I could realize that we had earned the victory,—bought it by the blood of those brave fellows whom I had seen lying in the cockpit of the *Lawrence*,—it was difficult to understand, even though we had fought so valiantly, how it all came about.

We were the victors in the first naval engagement fought on the lakes.

Commodore Perry had. earned for himself that fame and that glory which his brother predicted, and I was his brother's friend.

Alec, delirious with joy, flung his arms around my neck as one British ensign after another fluttered down from its masthead, and we two danced here and there over the blood-stained deck, unconscious almost, that we were making such an exhibition of ourselves, until we saw the sailors — old men bleeding from wounds that needed a surgeon's attention — hugging each other around the waist as they swung to and fro, cheering and yelling as if it were not possible to show their happiness save by movement and by noise.

The battle was ended, and Commodore Perry, Alec's

brother, was the one hero, to my eyes, among all who had proven their valor since the war began.

Here it is that my poor attempt at describing what befell my comrade and I while we served with Perry on Lake Erie, must come to an end, for the tale is done.

After a certain time I returned to my home at Presque Isle, and Alec accompanied his brother on what was little less than a triumphal tour to Washington.

Perhaps it is well to gather up the scattered threads of the story by explaining, what is most likely known to every one who shall chance to read these lines, that before sunset the *Little Belt* and the *Chippewa* were captured by the *Scorpion* and the *Trippe*, and brought to an anchor under the stern of the *Lawrence*.

It was hardly more than half an hour from the time our commodore left the flag-ship, and the dying men in the cockpit were sorrowing because of what seemed defeat, when he went on board again.

There, among all the evidences of what had well-nigh been a disaster, he received the swords of the Britishers who had been worsted in a fair fight wherein the odds were in their favor.

The *Lawrence* had lowered her flag ; but so hot had been the engagement immediately afterward that the enemy did not have an opportunity to take possession of her, and when we returned, for I accompanied Alec and our commodore, it was the same as if she had never submitted.

I have heard it said that never before had an American fleet or squadron encountered the enemy in regular line of battle, and never before, since England possessed a navy, had a whole British fleet been captured.

Even before we returned to our flag-ship, the commodore wrote on the back of an old letter this message to General Harrison, and sent it at once by special messenger : —

"We have met the enemy, and they are ours: Two ships, two brigs, one schooner and one sloop.

"Yours with great respect and esteem,

"O. H. PERRY."

[BY THE EDITOR.] It seems fitting that Master Dobbins's story should be concluded with the following extract from the "War of 1812," written by that eminent historian, Benson J. Lossing : —

"Then the ceremony of taking possession of the conquered vessels, and receiving the formal submission of the vanquished, was performed. Perry gave the signal to anchor, and started for his battered flag-ship, determined, on her deck, and in the presence of her surviving officers and crew, to receive the commanders of the captured squadron. 'It was a time of conflicting emotions,' says Dr. Parsons, 'when he stepped upon deck. The battle was won, and he was safe, but the deck was slippery with blood, and strewn with the bodies of twenty officers and men, seven of whom had sat at table with us at our last meal, and the ship resounded everywhere with the groans of the wounded. Those of us who were spared and able to walk, met him at the gangway to welcome him on board, but the salutation was a silent one on both sides; not a word could find utterance.'

"The next movement in the solemn drama was the reception of the British officers, one from each of the captured vessels. Perry stood on the afterpart of the deck, and his sad visitors were compelled to pick their way to him among the slain. He received them with solemn dignity and unaffected kindness. As they presented their swords, with the hilts toward the victor, he spoke in a low but firm tone, without the betrayal of the least exultation, and requested them to retain their weapons. . . .

"Vessels of both squadrons were dreadfully shattered, especially the two flag-ships. Sixty-eight persons had been killed and one hundred and ninety

x

wounded during the three hours that the battle lasted. Of these, the Americans lost one hundred and twenty-three, twenty-seven of whom were killed. Barclay, of the *Detroit*, the British commander, who had lost an arm at Trafalgar, was first wounded in the thigh, and then so severely injured in the shoulder as to deprive him of the use of the other arm. Finnis, of the *Queen Charlotte*, the second in command, was mortally wounded, and died that evening. . . .

"Perry's victory proved to be one of the most important events of the war. At that moment two armies, one on the north and the other on the south of the warring squadrons, were waiting for the result most anxiously. Should the victory remain with the British, Proctor and Tecumtha [1] were ready at Malden, with their motley army five thousand strong, to rush forward and lay waste the entire country. Should the victory rest with the Americans, Harrison, with his army in the vicinity of Sandusky bay, was prepared to press forward by land or water for the seizure of Malden and Detroit, the recovery of Michigan, and the invasion of Canada.

"All along the borders of the lake within sound of the cannon in the battle (and they were heard from Cleveland to Malden), women with terrified children,

---

[1] Tecumseh [ED.].

and decrepit old men, sat listening with the deepest anxiety; for they knew not but with the setting sun they would be compelled to flee to the interior to escape the fangs of the red bloodhounds who were ready to be let loose upon helpless innocency by the approved servants of the government that boasted of its civilization and Christianity. Happily for America — happily for the fair fame of Great Britain — happily for the cause of humanity — the victory was left with the Americans, and the savage allies of the British were not allowed to repeat the tragedies in which they had already been permitted to engage. . . .

"That victory led to the destruction of the Indian confederacy, and wiped out the stigma of the surrender at Detroit thirteen months before. It opened the way for Harrison's army to repossess the territory then surrendered, and to penetrate Canada. It was speedily followed by the overthrow of British power in the Canadian peninsula, and the country bordering on the upper lakes, and the absolute security forever of the whole northwestern frontier from British invasion and Indian depredations."

THE END.

With Preble at Tripoli

A STORY OF "OLD IRONSIDES" AND THE TRIPOLITAN WAR

By JAMES OTIS

349 pages. Cloth. 12mo. $1.50

Second Volume in "*The Great Admiral Series*"

It is a typical, dashing, instructive, and thrilling story. It is intended for boys, but there is hardly a person, young or old, who would not be intensely interested in it. Such a book as this should be welcomed by every parent.—*Boston Journal.*

This volume gives us a most vivid description of the exploits of the old "Constitution" and the brave men under Commander Preble's command. It is of the best juvenile literature.—*The Indianapolis Journal.*

It is a thrilling account of the loss of the "Philadelphia," and of the most famous "cutting out" party in our naval history. It adds a second volume to one of our most interesting series of books for young people.—*The Dial.*

The ever-stimulating account of "Old Ironsides" and her famous campaign against the Tripolitan pirates forms the basis of one of Mr. Otis's best stories; correct in its historical facts, interesting from beginning to end, it will be welcomed not only by the younger reader, but by the older one as well. —*The Presbyterian.*

WITH PORTER IN THE ESSEX

A STORY OF HIS FAMOUS CRUISE *in* SOUTHERN WATERS DURING THE WAR OF 1812.

By James Otis.

344 pages.   Cloth.   12mo. $1.50.

One of the best books that this favorite writer has ever penned, for it is full of life and vigor.— *Inter-Ocean.*

It is an ideal boys' story book and will inspire the youthful reader alike with patriotism and courage.— *Library Bulletin.*

The book is historically instructive and the story admirably told.— *Chicago Evening Post.*

Mr. Otis has a style peculiarly interesting to boys, and in this book he is up to his usual mark of excellence both as to accuracy of historical knowledge and fluency of narration. — *The Examiner.*

The events and issues of the war of 1812 have never received the attention they deserve at the hand of American students of history. This book will help to give life and reality to a subject at once thrilling and memorable in many ways.— *The Union.*

This story purports to be the personal experience of two boys, who enlist at the early age of fourteen, and who were with the *Essex* until the time of its capture. The book is sufficiently full of excitement to please boys, and while it pleases them it will also instruct them.— *The Intelligencer.*

BOSTON   W. A. WILDE COMPANY   CHICAGO

The Treasury Club

A STORY OF THE UNITED STATES TREASURY DEPARTMENT

BY

WILLIAM DRYSDALE

330 pp. Ill.   12mo.   Cloth, $1.50

First Volume in the United States Government Series.

This, the first volume in the United States Government Series, blends true information with an interesting story; it teaches and entertains at the same time.—*Congregationalist.*

It is an intelligently written narrative in story form, and will prove most interesting to all up-to-date young people. The idea of the book is both good in itself and most commendably worked out.—*Dial.*

"The Treasury Club" is a unique book, full of useful and valuable information. Parents will be glad to be able to get such a book as this to place in the hands of their children. —*Boston Journal.*

We welcome most heartily this most recent book by Mr. Drysdale. Should the subsequent volumes in this series be as entertaining as is this one, the entire set will be worthy of a high place among young people's books.—*The Standard.*

The underlying idea of the United States Government Series, of which this volume is the first, is a most excellent one. It is to give young readers an idea of the practical workings of the various departments of the United States Government, imparting special interest to the descriptions by putting them into story form. This volume. treating as it does of persons who may be seen to-day in and around the Treasury Department, and treating of facts gathered on the ground, is an exceedingly valuable addition to our young people's literature. Certainly it is a most useful, instructive, and interesting volume.—*Boston Transcript.*

TWO YOUNG PATRIOTS:

A STORY OF BURGOYNE'S INVASION.

By Everett T. Tomlinson, Ph. D.
12 mo. 366 pp. Cloth, $1.50. Ill.

"Two Young Patriots" takes up as its pivotal point, Burgoyne's invasion, and the narrative deals particularly with the historic events connected with the campaign. It not only gives to the reader a story, but also a most correct outline of the Invasion itself. The book is full of fervor, fire and fun, and its author here reasserts his claim to consideration as a high-class writer for first-rate books for boys.—*S. S Times.*

A story of Burgoyne's invasion. Indians and Indian warfare naturally have a very large place in these picturesque pages, and the reader will travel on through the book with breathless interest until he reaches the culmination of the story in the surrender of Saratoga.—*Book Buyer.*

A very shrewdly-planned campaign was Burgoyne's invasion, but it was equally shrewdly met by the colonists. Such is the basis of "Two Young Patriots," and the story loses nothing in the author's telling, for he has spared no pains with his historic accuracy, and it will doubtless convey to its readers a clearer idea of this pivotal point in the Revolution than they have ever enjoyed before.—*The Interior.*

It is exciting and thrilling, maintaining a strong interest throughout its pages. The make-up of the book is remarkably good, and the illustrations form a splendid addition.—*Journal of Education.*

A story of Burgoyne's invasion must take the boy reader by storm.—*Christian Endeavor World.*

CADET STANDISH OF THE ST. LOUIS

A STORY OF OUR NAVAL CAMPAIGN IN CUBAN WATERS.

352 pages. Cloth. $1.50.

In " Cadet Standish of the St. Louis " Mr. William Drysdale tells the story of an American boy to whom the Spanish war brought some novel and exciting experiences. The lad took part in the cable cutting off Guantanamo, the first exploit in which the great " merchant cruiser " distinguished herself. Not only is Mr. Drysdale an accomplished writer, but he has an intimate knowledge of the West Indian regions where most of the scenes are laid. The result is a most graphic and entertaining volume.—*Boston Journal.*

This is a story of the recent naval combat in Cuban waters. The book is picturesque and interesting from cover to cover. The local color is presented in a series of vivid touches and is skillfully interwoven with the narrative interest. The story is that of a young cadet on board the *St. Louis*, who is detailed for dangerous shore duty. His adventures make up the story that at once attracts and informs the reader.— *The Baptist Union.*

It is pleasant to be able to say that this tale of Cadet Standish is interesting, wholesome, natural, even among exciting scenes. The hero is a fine fellow in every way: in his relations to his widowed mother, as a young business man, and with his associates in the navy.— *The Literary World.*